Praise for Vicki Lewis Thompson

"*Cowboy Up* is a sexy joyride, balanced with good-natured humor and Thompson's keen eye for detail. Another sizzling romance from the RT Reviewers' Choice Award winner for best Blaze."
—*RT Book Reviews*

"Vicki Lewis Thompson has compiled a tale of this terrific family, along with their friends and employees, to keep you glued to the page and ending with that warm and loving feeling."
—*Fresh Fiction* on *Cowboys and Angels*

"Intensely romantic and hot enough to singe... her Sons of Chance series never fails to leave me worked up from all the heat, and then sighing with pleasure at the happy endings!"
—*We Read Romance* on *Riding High*

"If I had to use one word to describe *Ambushed!* it would be charming.... Where the story shines and how it is elevated above others is the humor that is woven throughout."
—*Dear Author*

"The chemistry between Molly and Ben is off the charts: their first kiss is one of the best I've ever read, and the sex is blistering and yet respectful, tender and loving."
—*Fresh Fiction* on *A Last Chance Christmas*

Dear Reader,

From the moment I was given a set of Lincoln Logs for Christmas many (cough, cough) years ago, I've had a thing for log cabins. I must have some pioneer blood in me because the idea of building a house by fitting notched logs together sounds brilliant. I've always longed to try it.

But I live in the desert, and mesquite trees are not log cabin material. So, next best thing, I was able to live out that fantasy while writing *Thunderstruck*. When you meet Damon, the cowboy who also knows his way around power tools, you'll realize I lived out a few other fantasies besides the log cabin one. Yes, this is a fun job, and don't let anybody tell you otherwise!

Thunderstruck is the second installment of my new series, Thunder Mountain Brotherhood, so maybe you picked up the first one, *Midnight Thunder*, which showed up last month. If not, no worries! Come meet the gang in this book and then go back to the other one. I'm sure you can navigate just fine, and I promise you're gonna fall in love with these cowboys. I have!

Yours in cowboy country,

Vicki Lewis Thompson

Vicki Lewis Thompson

Thunderstruck

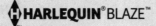

Recycling programs
for this product may
not exist in your area.

ISBN-13: 978-0-373-79855-1

Thunderstruck

Copyright © 2015 by Vicki Lewis Thompson

This edition published by arrangement with Harlequin Books S.A.

For questions and comments about the quality of this book, please contact us at CustomerService@Harlequin.com.

® and TM are trademarks of Harlequin Enterprises Limited or its corporate affiliates. Trademarks indicated with ® are registered in the United States Patent and Trademark Office, the Canadian Intellectual Property Office and in other countries.

Printed in U.S.A.

www.Harlequin.com

A passion for travel has taken *New York Times* bestselling author **Vicki Lewis Thompson** to Europe, Great Britain, the Greek isles, Australia and New Zealand. She's visited most of North America and has her eye on South America's rain forests. Africa, India and China beckon. But her first love is her home state of Arizona, with its deserts, mountains, sunsets and—last but not least—cowboys! The wide-open spaces and heroes on horseback influence everything she writes. Connect with her at vickilewisthompson.com, at facebook.com/vickilewisthompson and on Twitter, @vickilthompson.

Books by Vicki Lewis Thompson

HARLEQUIN BLAZE

Thunder Mountain Brotherhood

Midnight Thunder

The Sons of Chance Series

Long Road Home

Lead Me Home

Feels Like Home

I Cross My Heart

Wild at Heart

The Heart Won't Lie

Cowboys & Angels

Riding High

Riding Hard

Riding Home

A Last Chance Christmas

To get the inside scoop on Harlequin Blaze and its talented writers, be sure to check out blazeauthors.com.

All backlist available in ebook format.

Visit the Author Profile page at Harlequin.com for more titles.

To my sister and brother-in-law, Karen and David Santa Maria. I don't know the first thing about building a log cabin, but they know the first, second, third and probably the tenth thing! And they shared that knowledge, thank goodness.

1

FOLLOWING AN AFTERNOON of painting eaves, Damon Harrison was looking forward to a long shower and a cold beer. Southern California's current heat wave would make working at his foster parents' ranch in Sheridan, Wyoming, next week a treat. He peeled off his T-shirt as he walked into the master bedroom on his way to the shower.

This was the room he'd used almost exclusively while living in the house he was renovating. He kept the furnishings minimal—a queen bed on a metal rolling frame, collapsible shelving for his clothes, one floor lamp, a small TV and a computer desk on wheels so he could sit on the edge of the bed to type. He unfolded a TV table for meals.

When he began a renovation, he brought basic furniture, linens and kitchen supplies. All of it fit in his construction trailer once he was finished. Then he'd haul it to the next house and start all over again.

Damon loved flipping houses. He'd always gravitated toward construction work, and turning a trashed house into a showplace was immensely satisfying. The moment when he handed over the keys to the new owner gave him a rush of accomplishment that he hadn't found in anything else.

Passing the desk, he refreshed his laptop screen out of habit. Sure enough, there was an email from Phil Turner. Phil was a Sheridan carpenter who'd agreed to help him build a log cabin at Thunder Mountain Ranch over Fourth of July weekend.

Ordinarily, he preferred to work alone, but he could only spare a week to build the cabin, which wasn't enough time to do it right without help. His foster mother, Rosie, had recommended Phil, and Damon had exchanged emails with him for a couple of weeks. Phil was giving them a head start by ordering the materials and preparing the site.

After all their communications, Damon was confident they'd be on the same page and ready to go when he arrived in Wyoming. Working solo meant he hardly ever talked shop with anyone. Until now he hadn't realized he liked doing that.

He and Phil had discussed the project in depth. They'd settled on a concrete foundation, which would be poured today so it would be cured by the time he got there on July second. Phil seemed to have exacting standards, which made sense. After all, Rosie had recommended him.

When Damon arrived, the building permits would be approved and the electric box installed. All the materials would be on site, along with a rented forklift and a compressor. Phil had been good about sending pictures, so he'd probably emailed one of the concrete foundation.

Damon opened the email and downloaded the attached picture. The foundation looked perfect, exactly as he would have wanted it, with sill logs laid in squared-off precision around the perimeter to anchor the walls. The cabin wouldn't have any plumbing, the same as three others that had been built on Thunder Mountain Ranch years ago. No plumbing made construction a whole lot easier and cheaper.

Damon had been fifteen when he'd moved into the first cabin along with Cade Gallagher and Finn O'Roarke. About a year after Rosie and Herb Padgett had started a foster program at the ranch, they'd realized that their five-bedroom house would soon be bursting at the seams. Damon, Cade and Finn were the oldest boys and the ones who'd been at the ranch the longest, so they'd had the privilege of occupying the first cabin.

Remembering move-in day still gave him a charge. The three of them had been so excited, even though they'd had to trek out to a bathhouse instead of going down the hall like they'd been used to. The taste of freedom was far more important than indoor plumbing.

A couple of years before that, they'd sneaked into the woods at midnight and enacted a blood brother ceremony around a little campfire. They'd called themselves the Thunder Mountain Brotherhood—still did, in fact—and on that first night in the cabin they'd carved their TMB logo on a beam over the doorway. Good times.

But now Rosie and Herb had financial problems that could force them to sell the ranch. The Brotherhood, along with Cade's girlfriend, Lexi, had proposed launching Thunder Mountain Academy, a coed residential program for kids sixteen to eighteen who were considering a career involving horses. The seed money was being raised through Kickstarter, a crowdfunding program.

They'd decided a fourth cabin would allow them more housing flexibility when they began accepting students. Damon was the obvious person to build another one, and he was glad to do it. Initially, he'd budgeted two weeks, but the wrong tile had arrived for his current project and screwed up his schedule.

Good thing Phil had been available to supervise the critical first stages of construction. Damon studied the picture again. That must be Phil's shadow stretched across the troweled concrete. Damon wondered if Phil had long hair. Either that or he'd draped a bandanna over his head before putting on his hat to shield his neck from the sun.

Didn't really matter. Damon didn't care if a man had long hair or short if he could do the job. Judging from their email discussions, Phil was competent and thorough.

Clicking the reply tab, Damon crouched down and typed out a response.

Looks great. Never thought to ask. Can you work on the Fourth or do you have plans?

He doubted Phil was waiting for a reply. He'd put in a long day.

But as Damon started to leave, a click alerted him to an incoming email. Phil was probably catching up on email after work the way Damon usually did. With the hour time difference, Phil might have polished off his first beer already.

Assuming he was a beer drinker was a safe bet. Many construction guys were, and Phil seemed to fit the profile. Damon pulled the computer table over to the edge of the bed and sat down to read his reply.

I can work on the Fourth, but Rosie's planned a big barbecue for that night, so we might need to wrap things up by four or so.

Damon typed an answer.

Suits me. But I'll be watching my alcohol intake so I'll be bright and bushy-tailed on the fifth.

The reply was almost instantaneous.

Understood. He who drinks a fifth on the Fourth will not go forth on the fifth.

Damon chuckled.

LOL.

Then he added a more personal note because he was feeling so good about this collaboration.

It'll be great to finally meet you.

Same here. Well, I'm off to watch my favorite cop show.

Talk soon.

Damon sent the response and turned off the computer. Now that he'd heard from Phil, he didn't need to leave it on. This time crunch had played hell with his

social life, and he currently had zero women expecting
him to call, text or email. Just as well. Time to take that
shower, sip that beer and watch *his* favorite cop show.

PHILOMENA TURNER SMILED as she shut down her email
program and walked into her cozy kitchen to take the
tuna casserole out of the oven. Rosie had given her the
recipe last year and now she made it at least once a
week. Rosie was getting such a kick out of this plan to
show Damon Harrison that girls could be professional
carpenters, too.

Phil had helped trowel a slab of concrete today with
as much expertise as any of the men out there. Then
she'd operated the forklift when it was time to lay the
sill logs. But after a shower, she'd dressed in a floral
silk caftan for an evening at home. If Damon could see
the person he'd been emailing for two weeks, his jaw
would drop.

She agreed that the shock on his face when they met
would be fun to watch, but she wasn't surprised by his
assumption that she was a man. As the only child of her
widowed construction-worker dad, she'd spent all her
life around guys like Damon. His attitude was typical,
and Phil's choice of profession was not.

In some ways she felt a little sorry for him, but not
too sorry. According to Rosie he'd leaped to the conclusion that the local carpenter was a man even before hearing her name. She forgave people who made
that mistake when they called Phil's Home Repair and
thought she was the receptionist.

But to give the devil his due, Damon's idea of exchanging emails prior to his arrival had been brilliant.
Not only did they have the preliminary work on the

project finished, they'd also developed a mutual respect as professionals. Whatever blind spots he might have about the role of women in construction, he obviously knew his trade. Judging from his comments, he knew that she did, too. That would help erase any potential prejudices about women wielding power tools.

She dished out some casserole and poured the wine before taking both into the living room. Last year she'd refinished a coffee table that could be raised to dining table height. She refused to eat on a fold-up TV tray.

When she'd bought this cabin in the woods on the outskirts of Sheridan five years ago, the place had been a disaster both inside and out. It had sat empty for more than a year while varmints and weather had taken their toll. Now she could look around and feel pride in everything she saw.

The log walls had been recaulked. Because they were a foot thick, they didn't require insulation, but she'd replaced the single-pane windows and had hung a new door, a hand-carved beauty she'd found at an auction. New appliances, new bathroom fixtures and a bright blue galvanized metal roof had been pricey but worth it.

The rock fireplace had only needed to be cleaned out and capped to prevent critters from getting in. In winter she used it all the time, but in the summer she arranged dried flowers and pinecones on the grate to keep it from looking lonesome. Little touches like that made a house a home, and she'd loved feathering this nest, the first she'd ever owned.

The furniture was secondhand but sturdy. She'd refinished the wood and taught herself to reupholster anything that had a cushion. Because she'd worked so hard on each piece, they felt more hers than if she'd bought them new.

She'd chosen shades of green and blue because those were her favorite colors. Besides, a blue-eyed redhead looked good against a backdrop of those colors, so why decorate her home with something that clashed? She'd considered every aspect of this house carefully, from the area rugs on the wooden floor to the framed photos of the Big Horn Mountains on the walls.

After much inner debate, she'd bought a king bed. Ironically, she'd never shared it with a guy. She'd had two semiserious boyfriends since moving here, and in both cases she'd always ended up at the guy's apartment whenever they spent the night together.

Each had come up with a different excuse. One had insisted his bed was the best in the universe, and the other one had thought his shower was a great place for sex. She had a different theory, though.

Her construction abilities might be intimidating to some men, and her expertise was very much on display in this house. That insight had come after her last boyfriend had tried to talk her into selling her cabin and moving in with him. No, and hell no.

She'd begun to think of the cabin as a test to find out whether a man could accept who she was. So far she'd had no likely candidate to substantiate her theory. Damon certainly wouldn't qualify even though she had the distinct impression that Rosie was matchmaking.

Otherwise, why show Phil a bunch of pictures of the guy, who was surfer-boy gorgeous with his sun-bleached hair and laughing gray eyes? Phil appreciated nice abs and a great smile as much as the next woman. But according to Rosie, Damon avoided getting attached to anyone or anything, a trait Rosie had called a damned shame.

Phil loved Rosie, but not enough to tackle her fixer-upper of a foster son. House renovations were one thing. People renovations were a whole other issue, and Phil had no talent for it. Either a guy was right or he wasn't, and from all indications, Damon fell into Category B.

WAITING FOR CADE on the sidewalk outside the Sheridan airport felt like déjà vu, but at least the circumstances were better this time. Cade had picked Damon up less than a month ago when they'd all thought Rosie had suffered a heart attack. Fortunately, she'd had something not nearly so critical, a condition called broken-heart syndrome.

Apparently, the thought of losing Thunder Mountain Ranch had created symptoms very similar to a heart attack. Even though the diagnosis had been less dire, everyone who loved Rosie had vowed to do what they could to save the ranch. Consequently, Damon was flying to Sheridan for the second time this summer.

Cade pulled up in his trusty black truck, the same one he'd been driving for at least ten years.

Damon hopped in, dropped his duffel at his feet and grinned at his foster brother. "Are you and Lexi engaged yet, bro?" A month ago Cade had been reunited with Lexi, his high school sweetheart, but there were issues.

"Don't start with me." But Cade grinned back and offered his hand for the ritual Thunder Mountain Brotherhood handshake.

Damon closed the passenger door and buckled up. "I have your wedding present all picked out. I'm just waiting for Lexi to pop the question."

"Don't hold your breath." Cade tugged on the brim of his battered Stetson and put the truck in gear. "I had no idea what it was like waiting for someone to propose. Every guy should have to go through this, because let me tell you, it's hell."

"I'll bet. She still likes you, though, right?"

"Most of the time. But there's a lot I don't understand about women."

"I'm sure we could all say that." Damon knew for a fact that Cade and Lexi loved each other, but five years ago Cade had left town after telling Lexi marriage wasn't for him. Now he was back and ready to tie the knot but Lexi wanted to hold off.

"She might be waiting until after the Kickstarter deadline," Cade said, "to make sure Thunder Mountain Academy is a go before we make any plans. But September first seems like forever. I almost regret saying the decision was up to her. But I said it, so now I have to stick by it."

"Maybe you should take her to a fancy hotel in Jackson Hole, drink a bunch of champagne and talk her into it."

"That's either manipulation or coercion or both. Not doing it."

"So maybe I should talk to her and put the bug in her ear."

"Don't, bro. This has to be her idea. If you start making suggestions, you could mess things up."

Damon sighed and leaned back against the seat. "Then I'm out of ideas. I know how to get them into bed, but I've never tried to get them to the altar. I only have one piece of advice. Plenty of orgasms."

Cade laughed. "Got that covered."

"Then you're doing all a man can do."

"In fact, I spend most of my nights at her place, FYI."

Damon pretended dismay. "Are you telling me that I have to sleep in the Brotherhood cabin all by myself?"

"Ringo will keep you company. You might have to go get him, though. Now that he's settled in, he spends his nights in the barn hunting mice."

"Wouldn't want to deprive him of that pleasure." Damon had bonded with the gray tabby on his last trip. "But I'll definitely pay him a visit. I have a can of treats in my duffel."

"Have you adopted a couple of kittens like Lexi suggested?"

"Not yet. I'll see about it after I get back. No sense in getting them and then leaving for seven days."

"True."

"Any uptick in the Kickstarter contributions?"

"Some, but not as much as we'd like." Cade paused. "It's been suggested that I contact the Chance brothers and see if they'll put the word out."

"Who suggested that?" It had to be a touchy subject for Cade. Until last month he'd thought he was alone in the world except for his foster family. Then a cousin had shown up. Molly Gallagher Radcliffe, now married to a saddle maker in town named Ben Radcliffe, had informed Cade that he was related to her family in Arizona and the influential Chance clan over in Jackson Hole.

"Molly, for one. She's been at the ranch a lot to discuss the curriculum for the academy so the kids will get class credit."

"Yeah, we're lucky that she's a college professor and knows about these things. But she's a cousin to the

Chances just like you are. Why can't she tell them about the Kickstarter project?"

"She thinks that would make it seem like I don't have the cojones to say something, since it's a Thunder Mountain Ranch project, and I'm more directly involved than she is."

Damon took off his Ray-Ban sunglasses and massaged the bridge of his nose. "That makes sense, I guess." He put the glasses back on. "So who else is after you to buddy up to the Chances?"

"Lexi is, sort of. She figures they'd want to know because they're civic-minded and ready to help anybody, and there's a family connection through me, which makes it more likely they'd want to help. I admit that's a good point, but she's not pushing me to do it."

"Have you and the Chances talked at all?"

"Not yet. But I promised Lexi I'd go with her when she conducts a riding clinic over there on the fifteenth."

"That's less than two weeks away."

"It sure as hell is, and I still don't know what to do. That would be the time to mention Thunder Mountain Academy if I'm ever going to, but…"

"I get it." Damon wondered if anyone who hadn't been a foster kid would, though. "You don't want to meet them and immediately ask a favor."

"Right." Cade blew out a breath. "But I finally called Molly's dad last week because I thought I should start with Molly's side of the family. So here I was on the phone with an uncle I've never met, and we're talking about my mom dying, and he starts to cry."

"Shit."

"Yeah. Can't blame him. She was his sister, but I

got choked up, too. I thought I was over it. It's been fifteen years."

Damon nodded in understanding. "Stuff can come back to bite you. I still have that same nightmare. Not as much, but I had it again last week."

"Yeah, sometimes I have bad dreams about my dad, too." As Cade left city traffic and continued on to the highway that would take them to the ranch turnoff, they stopped talking. Damon appreciated that about his brothers. They all had demons of one kind or another, and they sensed when to end the chitchat and devote some time to just being quiet.

Cade had his load to carry. Abandoned by his abusive father, he'd lost his mother to cancer. By then his mom had changed all their records from Marlowe to her maiden name of Gallagher. Cade had assumed her family had turned their back on her, but really she'd been too ashamed of her situation to notify her family of her illness. Now Cade had suddenly been thrust into two extended families, which could be good once he got over the awkward parts.

Damon had no illusions that he was connected to any reputable families. He'd run away at twelve and had concocted an elaborate story that had landed him a temporary home with the family of a kid he'd known at school. By the time CPS had been called in, his parents had left town without a trace, probably relieved that he was gone.

In his recurring nightmare, he was a kid barely existing in the pigsty of whatever cheap housing his parents had found. While they were passed out drunk, he searched the cupboards for something to eat, and nothing was ever there. He woke up shaking and sweating.

When he'd lived in the cabin with Cade and Finn, they used to tell him jokes until he'd settled down. And they'd always kept snacks around for those times, too, because he'd wake up starving even if he'd had a good dinner that night.

To calm himself these days, he got up and walked around whatever house he was renovating. He kept his surroundings neat. He put away his tools, swept up sawdust and closed paint cans at the end of every day. He always had food in the cupboard, too.

Eventually, Cade broke the silence. "Did you ever go to that shrink Rosie recommended, the one the county would pay for?"

"Once. She was okay, but I got more mileage out of mucking out stalls. Did you go?" As close as they were, it was the kind of thing they would have kept to themselves.

"Yeah, five years ago after Lexi and I had our big fight about getting married. Nice lady, and she gave it to me straight. She said marriage would probably be a mistake until I had a better handle on who I was and what I wanted out of life. She was right."

"I'm sure she was, but at the time I was royally pissed at you for running out on Lexi. Poor girl was a basket case."

"And now she says I did her a favor."

Damon chuckled. "The woman has attitude. Is she coming to dinner tonight?"

"Yep."

"Good. And Rosie told me she'd invited Phil so we can meet each other before we start work in the morning."

"Yep."

"What's your take on Phil?"

"Um…" Cade paused to clear his throat. "I'd rather not say."

Damon stared at him. "What do you mean, you'd *rather not say*? Don't you like him?"

"Look, I can't talk to you about Phil without breaking a solemn promise to Lexi, and I'm not gonna do that."

"Why in God's name would you make such a promise?"

"Can we change the subject?"

"Is he an escaped felon?"

"No."

"Undocumented alien?"

"No. Did you notice the wildflowers along the road? They're spectacular this summer. I don't think I've ever seen—"

"Screw the effing wildflowers! Is he gay? I'll bet that's it, and if you all think I'm too prejudiced to work with a gay man, you'd be dead wrong. That's not an issue with me, so—"

"Phil's not gay."

"Then what's the problem?"

"There's no problem."

"If there's no problem, why are you dancing all around the subject?"

Cade sighed. "I knew I should've had Lexi pick you up."

"If you'd sent Lexi to fetch me, I would have known for sure something was fishy."

"Yeah, but Lexi's better at handling things like this than I am."

Damon rolled his eyes. This was going to drive him

crazy. "I have half a mind to invoke the Brotherhood oath."

"Please don't. Then I'm caught between betraying the oath and betraying Lexi. My head will explode."

"I just bet it would, too, honest as you are. Which is why I won't do that to you."

"Damon, it's nothing bad."

"It better not be."

"We're almost there. In about two minutes this discussion will be irrelevant. Admire the wildflowers until we get there."

Scowling, Damon glanced out the window. He had to admit that the purple, yellow and occasional splashes of red along the road made a pretty picture this time of year. But what was the deal with Phil?

Cade pulled into the circular drive in front of the rambling house where Damon had spent the happiest years of his life. Fourth of July bunting hung from the porch railing as it did every year. This place gave him such a lift that he couldn't imagine not being able to come back here. The Kickstarter project just had to work.

Rosie and Herb must have been watching for the truck, because they came out on the porch to greet him. Leaving his duffel, he jumped out, pulled off his sunglasses and jogged up the steps to give each of them a big hug. Damn, but it was good to be home. He'd been at the ranch three weeks ago, but it seemed longer.

"Oh, and Phil's here," Rosie said.

"Great!" At last he'd solve the mystery. Tucking his glasses in the vee of his shirt, he looked past Rosie to the person standing in the open doorway. That sure wasn't Phil, so the guy must have stayed inside.

She was tall, maybe five-nine, and slim. Her shoulder-length red hair made him think of polished cherrywood, and the sprinkling of freckles across her nose and cheeks added a wholesome touch. In contrast, her full mouth would tempt a priest to forget his vows.

But her eyes were the most striking thing about her. They were the saturated blue of a Wyoming sky on a hot summer day. A shirt in the same shade had been a good choice on her part. He had to drag his gaze from hers. She was just that mesmerizing. She might be Phil's girl, though, so he'd have to be careful.

Her jeans and boots were the type everybody wore around here, but on her they looked especially nice. If this was Phil's girlfriend, Damon was impressed. The guy had excellent taste.

But when she walked forward, hand outstretched and mischief dancing in those blue eyes, he suddenly knew he'd been had.

"It's good to meet you, Damon." Her voice trembled slightly as if she might be holding back laughter. "I'm Philomena Turner."

2

PHIL UNDERSTOOD RIGHT away why Rosie had said Damon had his pick of women. His expression when he'd caught sight of her had been filled with enough warm masculine appreciation to coax a response from her normally unflappable libido. All the years she'd spent hanging out with construction guys should have made her immune to such glances. Instead, her hormones were dancing a spirited two-step.

His reaction when he'd realized who she was had been adorable to watch. His gray eyes, much more compelling in person than in the pictures Rosie had shown her, went wide with shock. His mouth dropped open, and his handsome face turned red under his tan.

His deep voice, which she'd liked the minute she'd heard it, grew husky with embarrassment, which made him sound sexy as hell. "I had no idea."

"Gotcha!" Rosie looked immensely pleased with herself.

Damon turned to her. "Mom, you tricked me! How was I supposed to know that a carpenter named Phil was a—"

"You didn't know her name when you jumped to conclusions." Rosie smiled in obvious triumph. "That information came later in the conversation."

"But hearing it convinced me even more! Why didn't you correct me?"

Phil began to feel sorry for the poor man, but she was a bystander in this drama.

Fortunately, Herb came to the rescue. "She wanted to make a point, son." He put his arm around Damon's shoulders, which required him to reach up a ways. "She wanted to stretch your mind a little, challenge some of your preconceived ideas."

"Which I did." Rosie couldn't seem to stop grinning.

Damon's gaze swung to Phil. "You had to be in on this. You never dropped the slightest hint. The whole time we were emailing, you sounded like a guy discussing a construction project."

Okay, so maybe she shouldn't feel sorry for him. He might be gorgeous, but he could be in need of an attitude adjustment. "And how would a woman sound when she discussed that topic?"

He shrugged. "I'm not sure since I don't normally discuss construction with ladies. Just…different."

Phil got it now. Obviously, Rosie had been justified in playing this little trick. "Maybe you're imagining something like this." She modulated her voice to make it softer and more tentative. *"Gee, I can't decide whether we should order the eight-inch-thick logs or the twelve-inch. What do you think? You have way more experience than I do."*

His jaw firmed. "That's ridiculous. I don't expect women to defer to me."

"How about women carpenters?" She held his gaze.

Defiance flashed in his eyes. "Not them, either."

She wasn't sure she believed him. Before this little trick, he might have expected her to let him be in charge. Now he wouldn't dare. "Good. We should get along just fine."

Herb clapped his hands together. "Glad that's settled! Who's ready for a drink?"

"I'll take a beer," Cade said. "Lexi had a riding student this afternoon, but she should be here any minute."

Rosie linked her arm through Phil's. "Let's go toast the construction of Cabin Number Four. I chilled a bottle of that dry white you like."

Damon frowned. "You drink *wine*?"

"Do you have a problem with that?"

"No, but I thought you drank beer."

"Once in a while I do, but when someone offers a good white wine, I'll take that any day."

Damon waved a hand in the air. "Don't mind me. I'm still adjusting to the new reality." His smile seemed a little forced. "You guys go ahead with happy hour. I'm going to mosey down to the construction site before it gets too dark to see how it looks."

After growing up around testosterone-driven males, she knew that statement for what it was—an excuse that would allow him to retreat, lick his wounds and nurse his grievances. But she wasn't going to let him brood and build up a potential cache of resentment.

"I'll go with you." The trap had been sprung, and he'd been set back on his heels. But they'd be working together for the next week, and the rapport they'd established through emails was probably shot to hell. She should have anticipated that.

"Okay." He didn't sound eager to have her tag along.

That was to be expected. She'd just helped deceive him, so she'd have to work to win back his trust. He probably deserved the comeuppance. She didn't know him well enough to say for sure. Guaranteed he had some outdated ideas about women's work and men's work, but so did a lot of guys. She hoped that wouldn't interfere with this project.

"Don't be long," Rosie said. "Don't want you to miss my famous pot roast."

"Wouldn't dream of it." Damon gave her a more genuine smile before turning to Phil. "Ready?"

"Yep."

He didn't say anything as they started walking out to the meadow. The earth was spongy from the previous night's rain, and they had to detour around a couple of muddy spots. The three existing cabins followed a curve that would be a complete half circle when the fourth was built. The bathhouse stretched in a straight line behind them.

"I hope you know that Rosie loves you to pieces," Phil said at last, to break the ice.

"I know." He didn't look at her as he kept walking.

But she could almost hear him thinking, so she waited to see if he'd open up.

Finally, he let out a breath. "And it was a pretty harmless trick. God knows we had practical jokes going all the time when I lived here. Cade had an endless supply of rubber snakes, and I was the master of short-sheeting a bed. We put jalapeño peppers in each other's food and glued the toilet seats shut. Whatever prank you can think of, we probably did it."

"But?" She suspected there was more to that little speech.

"But I thought of you as a friend. And now you're... you're a woman."

She couldn't help laughing. "It sounds as if those two things are mutually exclusive in your world."

"Well, no, but..." His voice trailed off as if he couldn't find the right words.

"I'm not trying to defend what Rosie and I engineered, but what if you'd known all along that I was a woman? Would you have felt as confident putting me in charge of the foundation, the wiring and the permitting?"

His hesitation supplied the answer.

"Look at all we accomplished before you ever arrived!" She stepped onto the foundation, which gave her an inch or two advantage over him. She was amused when he immediately climbed up on it, too.

Tarp-covered, numbered piles of twelve-inch logs were stacked nearby. A forklift stood ready to move them into position. Everything else was here, too—windows, the front door, roof beams and the hunter-green metal roofing that would match the other three cabins. Power tools and rolls of ceiling insulation were stored in the second cabin because Damon would be staying in the first one.

"You've done a great job." He gazed at her.

"I'm glad you approve. Not to brag, but we had a hard rain last night, and you notice there's no evidence of water pooling anywhere on this slab."

"I did notice that. Who did the trowel work?"

"The guys from Rocky Mountain Concrete and Excavating. And me."

He nodded slowly, as if absorbing that. "So your name's Philomena, huh?"

"It was my mother's middle name."

"Was?"

"She died when I was a toddler."

"Oh. I'm sorry."

"I don't really remember her. My dad always says he loves me twice as much since I only have him."

"He's in Sheridan?"

"No, Cheyenne."

"Hmm." Damon studied her as if trying to decipher a confusing blueprint.

"The point is, I'm qualified to handle the site preparation, but I'm not sure you would have believed that if you'd been dealing with Philomena instead of Phil."

He sighed and ran his fingers through his sun-streaked hair. "Maybe not. I don't know a lot of lady construction folks, especially ones who are the owner of the company."

"It's not a very big company. I'm the only person in it."

"Even so, I'm impressed."

"Thank you." She looked into his eyes and fought the visceral tug she'd experienced when they'd met. Maybe her attraction to him was partly Rosie's doing. He'd had a lot of advance billing, and Phil had thought she was taking it all with a grain of salt.

Now she wondered if Rosie's sales pitch had worked like a charm. She couldn't deny that Damon Harrison turned her on. Standing here in the meadow surrounded by fragrant pines and wildflowers, she could still distinguish his unique scent. The combination of soap, a woodsy aftershave and a pheromone-laden male aroma excited the hell out of her. She'd only touched him once, when they'd shaken hands, but she wanted to touch him again.

No doubt his skin would be warm and humming with excitement, just like hers. He was one virile specimen, and she was as susceptible as the next woman. Perhaps more so, because she'd been depressingly celibate for the past year.

Sometimes life worked out that way. First you had the dry spell when no eligible males showed up, and then Fate played a joke and brought you a guy who oozed sexuality but had no intention of settling down. She didn't kid herself that she'd be the woman to change his mind. That kind of thinking led to disaster.

His chest heaved. It was a chest worth contemplating, but she made herself concentrate on his words.

"Listen, Phil." He sounded endearingly earnest. "I realize that you being a woman shouldn't change anything, but for me, it changes everything."

"I don't know why it should." She was bluffing. She knew exactly what he meant. They weren't just a man and a woman working on the same construction project. They were attracted to each other and they were both aware of it.

"You know why it matters."

She swallowed. "Okay, I do."

"I'm supposed to view you as another professional, and I'll try my best to do that, but you're…you're beautiful. And I have to ask, because it's in my DNA, is there some boyfriend or fiancé who'll clean my clock if I make inappropriate advances?"

"Not at the moment." She was having trouble catching her breath. "Are you going to?"

"Going to what?"

"Make inappropriate advances."

"Do you want me to?" He took a step closer.

"I don't know yet." She sucked in a lungful of air. "I need to think about that, which I can't do when you're standing there telling me I'm beautiful."

He smiled. "Just stating a fact, ma'am."

Oh, dear God. She could eat him up with a spoon. "I'm going…" She pointed back toward the house. "Back." Damn, she couldn't even talk right. If she didn't vamoose right this minute, she'd do something totally out of character, like grab him and plant a kiss on that smiling mouth.

"I'll go with you."

"No!" She backed away. "I mean, you should stay here and…and inspect the site. That's what you came out here for, right?"

"I came out here to get my bearings."

"Okay, but you can still inspect the site. You haven't really looked at it."

He didn't let up on that devastating smile. "Too busy looking at you."

"That's why I need to leave. See you at the house." She hopped down from the cement slab and speed-walked back to safety. She wanted to run, but then she'd be out of breath and chances were everyone was sitting on the porch with their drinks. Good thing the cabins weren't in view of the porch.

Sure enough, there they sat—Rosie, Herb, Cade and Lexi all relaxing in natural-finish Adirondack chairs. Rosie was the first to throw out a comment. "Don't tell me you had a fight already."

"Heavens, no." Her cheeks felt warm, but everyone was used to seeing her blush. It was what redheads did.

"He just wanted to walk around the site some more, and I was getting thirsty."

"Let me take care of that." Herb left his chair and crossed to the metal ice chest that always made an appearance during happy hour on the porch. "Have a seat."

"Thank you." She knew better than to argue about being waited on. For as long as she'd been coming out to Thunder Mountain to handle routine maintenance, Herb and Rosie had treated her more like a guest than a worker. They always offered food, drinks and conversation. Consequently, they were clients who'd turned into friends.

She sat down in one of the two empty chairs positioned beside Lexi. Obviously someone, probably Rosie the matchmaker, had set things up so that Damon would take the other chair. She was determined to be in control of herself when he arrived.

Herb handed her a chilled glass of white. Wiry and fit, he'd had a long career as an equine vet and seemed excited about teaching some basic skills to the teens they hoped to attract to the new program.

"You know, I just thought of something." Herb gazed down at her with those kind eyes that had inspired confidence in both humans and animals for years. "You could have built that cabin without Damon, so—"

"I could have, but it'll be faster with both of us working. And he wants to do this. I never once thought you should have hired me to do it alone. He won't charge a dime, while I plan to take full advantage of the riding lessons Lexi's offered me in exchange for my efforts."

"I certainly hope so." Lexi smiled. "You've been talking about learning to ride ever since I met you."

"And I never seem to find the time or the money.

This eliminates the money issue, so I'm determined to make the time right after Damon and I finish the cabin." As she said that she reminded herself not to ignore the fact that he'd head back to California in seven short days.

Normally she wouldn't consider getting involved with a guy who was here today and gone tomorrow. But whether it was due to Rosie's influence or not, she'd been hit hard by his first appreciative glance. And that unrehearsed speech about her beauty hadn't come across as a line.

A man like Damon didn't need a line to get a woman into bed. He had the kind of sexual potency that obliterated logic and caution. If she spent too much time thinking about the way he'd smiled at her, she'd end up knocking on his cabin door tonight.

"Phil?"

With a start she realized Rosie had spoken to her. "What?"

"Do you think that you and Damon will be able to work together?"

"Sure." It was the answer she was supposed to give, but privately she wondered if they'd end up sneaking off to have sex in the woods, which would seriously impact the schedule.

"If you have any doubts, we can still call Gerald. He's not as good a carpenter as you are, but—"

"You won't have to do that. Damon and I will be fine." She flinched at the idea of Gerald taking over. He was a nice enough guy, but he was sloppy. He didn't charge the hourly rate she did, but given his lack of expertise, he shouldn't.

Damon would hate working with Gerald. The job

would end up taking longer because Damon would have to fix whatever Gerald screwed up. Phil's work would pass muster, assuming she could keep her mind on it.

She *would* keep her mind on it. The project was too important to allow an inconvenient case of lust to interfere. And speaking of lust-inducing men, here he came.

Even his walk was sexy, the rat. He'd managed to locate an old straw cowboy hat, and if he'd been irresistible before, now he was deadly.

"I see you found your hat," Cade said.

"Picked it up when I went down to the barn to pay a social call on my old pal Ringo." He climbed up on the porch and grabbed a beer from the cooler. "That's some cat you have, Gallagher. He remembered me."

Phil didn't doubt it. Who wouldn't remember this guy?

"Don't let it go to your head." Cade sipped his beer. "He remembers anybody who brings him kitty treats."

"Yeah, but I didn't have them with me. They're still in my duffel." Damon twisted off the cap and took a swig of his beer. "He came right over."

"So he gave you the benefit of the doubt this time. Keep showing up without treats and see what happens."

"He's my buddy. He'd come to see me." Damon glanced at the Adirondack chair next to Phil. His gray eyes sparkled. "Excuse me, ma'am. Is this seat taken?"

"Be my guest." Oh, yes, he was charming, and she was more of a sucker for his brand of charm than she'd ever imagined.

"We never drank that toast to Cabin Number Four," Rosie said. "We should do it now."

"Absolutely." Damon raised his bottle. "To Cabin

Number Four and the success of Thunder Mountain Academy."

"Hear, hear!" Herb lifted his bottle, and everyone else on the porch did the same.

After they'd all taken a drink, Damon leaned forward so he could see around Phil. "Catch me up on what's been going on. Cade said the contributions weren't coming in as fast as we need them to."

"They'll pick up," Herb said. "It's only July, and we have until September first to raise the money."

Phil had only recently learned how crowdfunding worked. "It still doesn't seem fair to me that you either meet the goal or all the money goes back to the contributors. Isn't there any wiggle room on that?"

"Not really." Rosie was looking much better these days. The color had returned to her face, and she'd resumed her regular trips to the beauty salon to have her silver roots tinted their original blond. "That's the way we set it up. A flexible deadline makes us look as if we're not sure the project will succeed. It's better if you state the amount you need and you either get it and the project is funded, or you don't and the money's all returned."

"There's a risk factor." Herb looked at Phil. "But that's true of anything. You took a risk moving here from Cheyenne to open Phil's Home Repair."

"I guess so." But if she'd failed, no one else would have suffered. If the Kickstarter program for Thunder Mountain Academy failed, the ranch would be sold. Herb and Rosie would lose the place they loved, and so would all the foster boys who had been sheltered here.

"It's going to work," Damon said. "I feel it in my bones. We have so many elements to offer kids who are considering a career with horses—equine vet experience from Dad, a riding program designed by Lexi, saddle making taught by Molly's husband, Ben, and horse training taught by our favorite singing cowboy."

"Don't make fun," Cade said.

"I'm not! Rosie said you tamed that black gelding of yours by singing to him." Damon turned to Phil. "Did you hear about that?"

"I did."

Cade sipped his beer. "It makes a good story, but it wasn't quite that simple."

"Maybe not, but I couldn't have done it." Damon glanced over at Phil again. "See, I can't carry a tune in a bucket. If I tried singing to a horse he'd likely buck me off and then trample me to shut me up."

She laughed. "I doubt it's that bad."

"No, he's right," Cade said. "He's terrible. But lucky for you, bro, Hematite is gentle enough now that you can ride him without singing."

"You'll let me ride him?"

"I will if you're nice."

"I'm always nice."

Of course he had to say it in that low, sexy voice of his. Phil resisted the urge to fan herself. He might not be a good singer, but she had no trouble imagining that husky voice murmuring to her as they made long, slow love in her refinished sleigh bed. Oh, he'd be nice, all right. Very nice.

And for once, she wouldn't have to worry about a man being intimidated by the evidence of her construction skills. Damon might appreciate the effort she'd put into her home. She'd have fun showing it off to someone who understood how many hours she'd spent on it.

But in order to do that, she'd have to invite him there. And she knew as sure as her name was Philomena Hermione Turner that once she had that man in her house, she would eventually have him in her bed. So before she issued her invitation, she'd better be damned sure that was what she wanted.

3

THROUGHOUT HAPPY HOUR and dinner, Damon's mind ran laps like a hamster on a wheel. He'd never had a problem like this. Because he flipped houses and operated alone, he'd never had to worry about mixing business with pleasure.

But here was Philomena Turner with her incredible blue eyes, sexy mouth and lithe body. She was in great shape because she worked her muscles hard just like he did. Now that he was over the shock, knowing that they had essentially the same job might be the most intriguing thing about her.

He envisioned what she'd look like all flushed and sweaty after a day spent using power tools in the heat of a Wyoming summer. Then he stopped thinking about it before he embarrassed himself by getting a woody. If she'd shut him down and made it clear she wasn't interested, that would have helped. He'd never believed in chasing women who played hard to get.

Instead she'd traded smoldering looks with him in the meadow, and during dinner he'd caught her glancing his way several times. He had no trouble interpreting what those glances meant. She was considering having sex with him. To make matters worse, he was considering having sex with her, too.

That was probably a really bad idea. He had a hunch that Rosie had intended this all along. She'd put them next to each other at dinner around the cozy kitchen table and had kept tabs on them throughout the meal. She was convinced her boys should all settle down with nice women.

She'd be overjoyed if he became seriously involved with Phil, but he'd earn a bunch of demerits if they only had a casual fling. So the best solution to this mess would be finding someone else to help him build the cabin.

Cade was available, but he'd never shown the slightest interest or aptitude for construction. By the time the second and third cabins had gone up, Damon had been working alongside the adults and loving every minute. Cade had smashed his thumb with a hammer and sliced his arm with a handsaw before he'd finally been sent off to groom the horses, instead.

Too bad the old guy who had helped construct all three cabins wasn't available, but he'd retired long ago. There had to be somebody else in town who would work cheap, though. He'd better have a heart-to-heart with Phil, explain the problem and get her to recommend someone.

He'd talk to her after dinner. They all had coffee and were finishing generous servings of apple pie à la mode—Rosie had made Damon's favorite dessert and he'd thanked her for it. She really did love him, just like Phil had said.

Rosie also might think she knew what would make

him happy. He'd learned that people tended to want for others what they'd always wanted for themselves, without taking differences into account. Maybe during this trip he'd find a private moment to explain to Rosie why flipping houses suited his personality while marriage and a permanent home did not.

When the meal was over, he got up and started clearing the table the way he always had. Rosie understood that about him, at least, and had never tried to talk him out of helping. She'd taught the other boys to pitch in during kitchen duty, but Damon had done it without being told.

Clutter bothered him, but dirty dishes drove him nuts. He didn't have to worry about that with this group, though. With everyone helping, the dishwasher was loaded and the table wiped down in minutes.

"I have a case of Baileys in the pantry if anyone wants more coffee with a little kick to it," Rosie said.

Damon exchanged a grin with Cade. The two of them had bought her the booze when she'd been laid up in the hospital. She'd forbidden anyone to bring her flowers because that would imply she was seriously ill. So instead they'd delivered a case of Baileys to her hospital room. She'd gotten the message—she'd have to live a long time in order to drink it all.

"Thanks for the offer," Phil said, "but I should probably head on home."

That was his cue. "Before you leave, could I talk to you for a minute?"

"Sure." She walked over to him as if she expected him to blurt it out right here in the kitchen, in front of everybody.

"Let's go outside."

She blinked. "All right."

He was aware of Rosie's little smile and Cade's lifted eyebrows. Ignoring their reaction, he ushered Phil out of the kitchen, through the living room and out the front door. Let them think what they liked. He was taking steps to end this potentially explosive situation.

She stopped on the porch. "Okay, we're outside. What is it?"

"Let's take a walk down to the barn."

"Why?"

"Look, I'm not going to jump you, if that's what you're worried about." Not that it hadn't crossed his mind, but he was a more disciplined man than that.

She smiled. "I doubt that's your style. I picture you getting a woman alone and then charming her until she jumps *you*."

"That's not my plan, either." Damn, but she looked good with the porch light gleaming on her red hair. "Believe it or not, I have something important to discuss, and I don't want to do it where someone might come out and interrupt what I have to say."

"Everyone in the kitchen thinks something is going on between us."

"Well, it's not, and if I have anything to say about it, it won't."

"Oh, really? When did you—"

"Let's walk. We can go see Ringo." He gestured toward the porch steps, and to his relief, she started down them.

"I've met Ringo a couple of times. He really is a great cat."

"And a smart cat, too. He stowed away in the truck

when Cade left Colorado to drive up here. He knew who to hook up with for a better life."

"Cade's a good guy. I wasn't sure I'd like him after hearing how he'd run out on Lexi, but now that he's back it looks like they're resolving that situation."

"I hope so. Those two belong together."

"Seems like it." She stopped and turned to him. "Okay, nobody can hear us unless we start shouting. Do you really want to pay Ringo a visit or can we just settle whatever's bugging you right here?"

"I guess we can talk here." He reached for his hat to tug the brim down, but he'd left it in the living room. Instead he shoved his hands in the pockets of his jeans, and that was where they were going to stay. "We need to find you a replacement."

"Is that right?" She tucked her hands in her hip pockets and rocked back on her heels to look at him. The gesture emphasized the swell of her breasts under her blue shirt. "And may I ask why?"

"You don't know?" Even now, with his plan foremost in his mind, he wanted to grab her and find out what that tempting mouth of hers tasted like.

"Not for sure. Spell it out for me."

"I've tried to imagine us working together, and it always turns out the same way in my mind."

"Which is?" A couple of dusk-to-dawn lights kept the inky darkness at bay, but didn't make the area bright enough to see faces clearly.

That was just as well, in his estimation. He didn't need to look into her eyes and discover they were hot with desire. "We end up having sex."

"You could be right."

He couldn't see it in her eyes, but he sure as hell

heard it in her voice. His fingers curled inside his pockets, and his groin tightened. In any other scenario, he'd haul her into his arms and the game would be on. "We can't do that."

"I can't speak for you, but I'm fully capable of doing that."

He blew out an impatient breath. "I didn't mean we *can't*, like we aren't physically able." He was *so* physically able. More so with every passing second. "I mean it wouldn't be good."

She chuckled.

"I didn't mean that, either, damn it! Let me just say this. Rosie set us up."

"I figured."

"So we agree on that. Good. The thing is, in Rosie's world, people fall in love and get married. If she figures out we're seeing each other, then that's what she'll expect, but that's not what I'm prepared to deliver, so the best plan is to find your replacement."

"Whoa there, cowboy. Back up the forklift. How did we get from *I'm not marriage material* to *you have to be replaced*? I think you missed a few key points in the middle."

He thought through what he'd said. She was right that he'd skipped over the embarrassing part, which was that he didn't trust himself to work with her, especially knowing that she'd be fine with getting horizontal. "I don't..." He paused to scrub a hand over his face. "I don't think I can resist you."

She didn't respond.

"Did you hear me?"

"Oh, yes, I heard you. I'm just savoring that last comment. I may have aroused uncontrollable lust in a man before, but he's never admitted it. I'm having a Cleopatra moment, a Helen of Troy moment, a Marilyn Monroe moment, a—"

"Okay, okay. Let's get back to the heart of the matter. Who can we call in to take over for you?"

"Nobody."

"Oh, come on, Phil. There has to be some guy who won't charge a fortune and can do the job."

"Not really. We need to be familiar with his or her work, because we can't be bringing some unknown person in on this deal. It's too important. That leaves the guy who built the original cabins and is now retired, you, me and Gerald Stiffle."

Damon groaned. "Stiffle would be a disaster. He was incompetent when I left, and I doubt he's turned into a master builder since I've been gone."

"He hasn't. I told Rosie he wasn't an option when she asked whether you and I could get along and accomplish the job. She was ready to take him on if necessary."

Damon watched his options disappear. "I can't work with Stiffle. I'd have to go behind him and check everything he did. He's okay for changing washers on faucets and junk like that, but even then, I'd worry."

"Which leaves you with me."

"Damn it." He couldn't keep watching the way her breasts swelled under her shirt with each breath, so he stared into the darkness. "Sure as the world I'm going to end up in trouble with Rosie."

"Would you like me to talk to her, woman-to-woman, and explain the predicament we're in?"

"No!"

"So you'll talk to her?"

"I… No. Not about us, anyway. I was planning to

explain to her sometime during this visit that flipping houses suits me, especially the way I do it. I live in the house until it's done and then move to the next one, which isn't a good lifestyle for a wife and family. I want her to give up on that idea because I like how I run my business and don't intend to change."

"So you could start with that discussion and segue into our particular circumstance. Then she'll know in advance that if we sleep together it doesn't mean anything."

That hit him wrong. "Wait a minute. It would mean *something*, just not—"

"Okay, bad choice of words. It wouldn't lead to love and marriage. Is that better?"

"It's better, but I have trouble picturing me having such a conversation with Rosie. For one thing, she won't believe me. I'm sure she's convinced that if the right woman comes along, I'll change my ways."

"She may think that, but I don't."

He stared at her. "You don't?"

"Why does that surprise you?"

His mind stumbled. "Don't most women think a guy just needs the love of a good woman to turn his life around?"

"I have no idea. Maybe. I grew up surrounded by my dad's working buddies. Some of them will never change, no matter what women get ahold of them."

"You should try telling that to Rosie. I guarantee she'd argue with you about it. Sure, she might give up on the really bad apples, like the SOBs who beat their kids or abandon their families, but if a man's decent, she wants to find him a soul mate."

"Like I said, that's her prerogative. But I don't believe it. If you tell me you're happy with your life as it is, I will believe you. I won't harbor some secret plan to convert you to domesticity."

"Huh. You're even more unusual than I thought."

"Probably. And now that we've had this deep discussion, I'm heading home. See you at dawn at the building site." She turned and started toward her truck.

"Wait." He followed her. "We haven't settled anything."

She turned back to him. "What's to settle? We have to work together unless you want to trade me for Stiffle."

"God, no."

"Then I'll be here at sunrise, and we'll see what happens."

He groaned. "Phil..."

"Look, I want to get this cabin built as much as you do. I love Rosie and Herb, and if Thunder Mountain Academy means they can live out their lives here, I want to do what I can to make that happen."

"So do I."

"Then man up, Harrison. We'll work our tails off during the day, and if the close proximity leaves us frustrated at quitting time, then we'll figure out what to do about that."

"You think like a man."

She smiled. "Spoken like a man who has a lot to learn about women."

At the moment he had no interest in learning about women in general, but he sure wanted to find out what made this particular one tick. And what made her moan and cry out with pleasure. He stood with fists clenched as he battled the urge to reach out. He itched to make contact.

Her voice softened. "My original plan was to keep our relationship strictly professional. Then I met you."

That admission snapped what little control he had. Grasping her shoulders, he pulled her forward and kissed her. It wasn't an elegant kiss. Desperation made him clumsy, and he landed off-center.

She adjusted the fit and…he was lost. Her mouth was perfect. He'd kissed more women than he could count, and yet he'd never settled into a kiss that felt so absolutely right. Even more perfect, she tasted of apple pie à la mode, his favorite dessert.

He kept his hands on her shoulders because if he let them stray, the kiss would turn into something else entirely. He didn't want that. For now, for tonight, he only needed the magic of his lips on hers.

They kissed as if they'd done this before, which was an eerie feeling. He explored with his tongue, and then she returned the favor. The sweet thrust of her tongue in his mouth jacked up his pulse rate. He knew how much he wanted her. To know that she wanted him was enough to make him forget all the complications this kiss would bring.

Gradually their breathing changed and became more labored. She eased away. "Not tonight," she murmured.

"I know." He released her because that was the right thing to do.

"We'll see how it goes." She backed toward her truck.

"Yeah." But he knew how it would go. He'd never kissed a woman that passionately without following through. They would be lovers. It was a done deal now.

He watched until her truck's taillights disappeared around a curve in the road.

"I waited until I heard her drive away before I came out here." Cade walked up beside him. "I need to apologize."

"Nah." Damon turned to him. "I see how it was. Rosie and Lexi ganged up on you. When a guy's sweetheart and his mom box him in, there's not much to be done."

"Even so, it's put you in a difficult position. I can tell you really like her, but if you do anything about it, Rosie will start planning the wedding."

Damon glanced at him. "You know all about that, don't you, bro?"

"'Fraid so. But if you're not ready for that kind of commitment, then—"

"I'm not. But you want to know the weird thing about this? Phil has no intention of trying to change me. She accepts that I'm a guy who isn't into the white picket fence routine. She's a-okay with a temporary arrangement."

"Wow, that's kind of different."

"I know, but *she's* different. She's strong and she's savvy. I've never met anyone like her. She grew up with guys like me and she has no illusions. She'd rather not be attracted to me, but she is."

"Nothing new there. That's the story of your life ever since you hit puberty."

"But Phil's so practical about it. Instead of trying to make this into something it isn't, she seems fine with having a great time for a few days and then going our separate ways."

"But then there's Rosie, who expects you to ride off into the sunset together."

"Yeah. So, um…" Damon rubbed the back of his neck. "Would you consider talking to her about Phil and me?"

Cade chuckled and shook his head. "Nice try. That's your job, and somehow you have to make it stick."

"Phil understands how it is with me. Why can't Rosie?"

"Because you're one of her boys. She has definite ideas about how our lives should turn out. She's a fixer. That was what got her into social work all those years ago, and what prompted her and Herb to turn the ranch into a foster home."

"We're damned lucky she's a fixer," Damon said. "She saved my bacon, that's for sure."

"She saved all of us, and she…well, she can't stop trying to help. She thinks matching you up with Phil was a stroke of genius, and before you go blaming it all on Rosie, it was Lexi's idea to start with."

"Wait, there's the plan! I don't know why I didn't think of it. I'll talk to Lexi, who should understand given that she's dragging her feet regarding you."

"Hey! Tender subject."

"Sorry. But see, I could talk to Lexi, and Lexi could talk to Rosie. How's that?"

"It would have sounded great to me when we were in junior high."

"Shit." Damon sighed. "You're right. I have to face Rosie, which will be damned embarrassing, and find a way to explain that Phil and I will be nothing more than friends with benefits."

"Can I hide in the closet and listen?"

"*No.* And if there's a rubber snake in my bed tonight

I swear I'll sneak over to Lexi's duplex and duct-tape the front door while you two are in there doing it. So watch yourself."

Cade just grinned at him. "It's good to have you back, bro. Let's go have another beer before we call it a night."

"Sounds fine to me, but Lexi probably wants to take you home and have her way with you."

"She probably does, but we need to drink another beer so she can slip out to your cabin and get rid of that rubber snake."

4

PHIL WAS USED to hard work, but she'd never had the mingled pleasure and pain of constructing a cabin with Damon Harrison. The man provided gorgeous scenery, but she barely got to enjoy the view because he never let up. She'd thought her dad was a dedicated construction guy, but Damon had him beat by a country mile.

They started building the walls at dawn, a process similar in principle to the old Lincoln Logs set she'd had as a kid. Except these logs required a forklift to transfer them from the correct pile to the section of the cabin where they belonged. She suggested taking turns driving the forklift and he'd agreed immediately.

In general she had no complaints, except the man seemed to have no Off switch. She was determined to work at least as hard as he did, so they kept up a steady pace. First they put down a layer of caulk along the flat side where the logs joined. After they positioned the next log, they drove spikes through predrilled holes to make sure the walls were rock-solid.

They ran the electrical wires between the logs for a cleaner look, and Damon's exacting measurements guaranteed they never drove a spike through a wire. When Phil had worked for her dad, they'd sometimes run into careless builders. She'd guessed from Damon's emails that he wasn't at all careless, but after the first few hours, she knew it for a fact.

Rosie brought them lunch at noon, and talking with her had been the only time Phil had been able to sit down all day. By the time they stowed the tools at six o'clock, they had walls that reached to her waist. At this rate Damon would be able to go back to California early if he chose to.

Any worries that she'd be distracted by the way his sweat-dampened T-shirt clung to his muscled chest or how his jeans cupped his firm ass when he leaned over to pick up a drill bit were pointless. She'd had no leisure time to enjoy those things, not unless she wanted to look like a slacker.

"Good." Damon took off his straw cowboy hat and mopped his face with a bandanna as he gazed at the walls rising from the foundation. "This was the height I wanted to reach today."

Phil stopped drinking water from a large jug and looked at him. "I didn't know you had daily goals for this project."

"It didn't seem necessary before, when I thought…"

"When you thought I was a man?" She was hot and tired and in no mood. "But with a woman you need daily goals? What the hell is that about?"

"Hey, hey, hey. That's not what I meant at all. You've worked faster and more efficiently than any guy I know. I'm blown away by what you can accomplish."

She was somewhat mollified. "So I guess you can

forget about the goal thing, now that you know I can cut it."

"Nope." He put on his sweat-stained hat. "I set up ambitious production goals to keep *me* on track. Thinking about the job last night, and knowing how you affect my concentration, I decided some benchmarks would help me stay focused."

"You didn't seem to lack concentration today." A breeze wafted through the meadow, and she fanned her damp T-shirt to take advantage of it. "I've never worked with anyone who concentrated on the job as hard as you do."

He gave her a long, slow grin.

"What?"

"Then I must have hidden it well." His smile widened. "Props to me."

"Hidden what well?"

"You didn't catch me watching you?"

"No."

"Excellent."

"When were you watching me?"

"A lot. Whenever you leaned over to spread the caulk, and especially when you drilled holes for the spikes."

"There's nothing sexy about using a power drill." Not true. Damon with a power drill would have been extremely sexy if she'd had the luxury of watching him.

"That's what you think. When you use the drill your breasts quiver."

That movement would have been subtle. He'd definitely been paying close attention. "I can't imagine where you found the time to notice things like that. I've been going full throttle all day and barely glanced at you."

"And consequently, I'm pretty sure you got more work done than I did."

"Really?" That was a gratifying thought.

"Yep, I'd bet on it. I have the feeling you were out to prove something to me today."

"I thought you were trying to prove something to me!"

"I was, but then you'd do something sexy and I'd forget about my macho image and stop working so I could stare at you."

"I totally didn't notice." No doubt because she'd been determined to show him that she could work rings around any man doing the same job.

"You were pushing pretty hard."

"We need to get this done." But that hadn't been her motivation.

His soft smile told her he knew that. "Let's make a deal to take it easier tomorrow."

"That's a given. It's the Fourth. We'll need to quit early so we can get cleaned up for the barbecue."

"Yeah, right. I forgot." He glanced at the water jug in her hand and held up his empty one. "Can I have some of that? I'm out."

"Sure. Let me pour you some."

"Not necessary." He set his jug on the wall. "I've kissed you, remember?"

As if she'd ever forget. But she'd pushed it to the back of her mind today to make sure she didn't lag behind. But now that kiss was all she could think about. He walked over, took the jug and tipped it up so he could drink.

Maybe if she hadn't been dazed by hours of physical

labor, she would have maintained her cool. Or not. He'd been staring at her all day so why not return the favor?

He was an arresting sight, and she couldn't manage to look away. She took it all in—the flutter of his blond lashes as his eyes drifted closed, his full lips circling the mouth of the jug, the tendons tightening on the back of his hand as he grasped the jug and the movement of his tanned throat as he swallowed.

He lowered the jug and glanced at her. His breath caught. "Good God, Phil. Don't look at me like that unless…"

"Unless what?"

"You want me to show up at your door tonight."

She held his gaze as her heart thumped in an urgent rhythm. She imagined him at her door, in her house, in her bed. "As it happens, I do want that."

"You're absolutely sure."

"Yes."

"Then count on it. I've been thinking about this all day, and I—"

"Hey, kids!" Herb's cheerful voice blasted through the mounting tension, scattering it.

He was quite a distance away, and Phil wondered if Rosie had cautioned him to make his presence known well in advance, in case something significant was taking place in the meadow. Turned out it had been.

Damon returned the greeting and stepped away from Phil. "Hey, Dad! Come see the progress we've made."

"Whoa!" Herb came close enough that he didn't have to shout. "You two accomplished a heck of a lot."

"Phil gets the credit. The woman's amazing."

"I think you're both amazing." Herb beamed at them.

"Rosie wants to know if you're ready for some lasagna, so she sent me to check on things."

Phil made a decision. "You know how I love Rosie's lasagna, but I'm sweaty and tired. I want to go home, take a cool shower and put on my silk caftan before I even think about food." She took satisfaction from Damon's quick gulp when she'd mentioned the silk caftan.

"I completely understand," Herb said. "Damon, do you want to hit the showers before dinner? There's time. Lasagna will keep."

"I definitely need to do that." Damon flicked a glance at Phil. "Enjoyed working with you today. Looking forward to the next round."

She smiled at him. "See you then." Could be tonight, could be at dawn in the morning when she returned to the building site. If Damon wanted to keep their potential rendezvous a secret from Rosie, he wouldn't have complete freedom of movement.

As she drove away, she realized he didn't know her address. He could probably get that from…someone. But then she thought of something else. He didn't have his own transportation. If he wanted to keep his visit on the down-low, he couldn't borrow Herb and Rosie's truck, so that left Cade's. She wasn't clear on how Cade and Lexi were working out their situation, so his truck might not be available, either.

Damon couldn't very well walk to her house, although he might be motivated enough to do that. The scenario was fun to contemplate but unlikely to happen. By the time she reached home, she'd decided the chances of seeing Damon tonight were slim to none.

Her routine wouldn't change much regardless, so she proceeded the way she always did on nights when she'd worked up a sweat doing her job. After a long, cool shower, she smoothed lotion over her tired muscles. Then she slipped into one of her three silk caftans, all in shades of blue and green.

In winter she wore flannel and slippers, but in summer she spent her evenings in caftans—and nothing else. The silk felt sensuous against her skin, especially without underwear.

Her dinner was a salad topped with fresh veggies. She opened a bottle of white wine. As she settled in front of the TV, she remembered to be grateful for the life she'd created even if she didn't have a special someone sharing it.

Even if Damon showed up, which he probably wouldn't, he'd only be around for less than a week. Maybe she'd be better off if he didn't come over tonight, or any night. She talked a good game, but she might not be as happy about the temporary nature of their connection as she'd said.

She *wanted* to be happy with it. Intellectually, she accepted the idea of taking pleasure where she could find it, specifically when no Mr. Right happened to be on the horizon. A woman had needs.

Logically, if she could release some of the tension from those needs with Mr. Wrong, she wouldn't be in deprivation mode if she met Mr. Right. She'd also be less likely to mistake Mr. Wrong for Mr. Right. Not everyone was as honest about their intentions as Damon.

He could have implied that he'd stick around if things worked out between them. A lesser man might have. She clicked off the TV show when she realized she'd lost the thread of the story. A little instrumental music suited her mood better tonight.

Humming with the music, she cleaned up her dinner dishes and poured herself a little more wine. Now that she'd sorted through her thoughts about Damon, she really, really wanted to see him tonight. But since he could be stuck at the ranch without wheels, she might just have to go to him.

Sex in a bunk bed wasn't as appealing as sex in a king-size sleigh bed, but it was better than nothing. She looked at her half-full glass of wine. She shouldn't have any more if she intended to drive back out to the ranch.

All right, she'd do it. She'd take the side road down to his cabin so nobody would see her arrive. He might still be up at the house with Rosie and Herb, but that was okay. She'd let herself in. The cabins were hardly ever locked.

She debated whether to get dressed, but the idea of greeting him in this very feminine caftan had been part of her mental image all along. She hated to give that up. Finally, she shoved her feet into flip-flops and grabbed her purse.

She was halfway out the door when she turned back. What a bummer if she went to all this trouble and he didn't have condoms. But she did. At one time she'd thought sex would actually happen in her sleigh bed so she'd bought a box. Never been opened.

It wouldn't fit in her purse, so she carried it out to her truck and tossed it on the passenger seat. If he had them, she wouldn't even mention these. She'd just bring them home.

Driving her truck in her caftan and no underwear felt daring, the kind of move she'd envision with a man like Damon. And being daring felt wonderful. She was so glad she'd changed her Fourth of July plans. Originally she'd intended to take the time off and go down to Cheyenne to see her dad and her stepmother, but then this project had come along and she'd canceled. She'd go another weekend.

Before her dad had started dating about six or seven years ago, Fourth of July had been a big deal for them. Her dad would always research the most spectacular displays within driving distance, and they'd pick one and be right there in the thick of the crowd. But then he'd met Edie, and things had changed.

Phil was happy for him, really happy. He'd waited until she was an adult before looking for a second wife, and he'd found a great one. Phil thought the world of Edie, but she didn't want to live in their house and be a fifth wheel. Moving to Sheridan and opening her own business had been the best thing for everyone.

If she'd stayed in Cheyenne, she certainly wouldn't be tooling down a country road in a silk caftan with no underwear on. But she wasn't in Cheyenne. She was driving toward Thunder Mountain Ranch to seduce a very hot guy, which called for some music. Punching the button on the radio, she lucked out with a tune she knew, so she belted out the lyrics.

She was in the middle of the chorus and moving with the beat, when her truck's headlights caught the glow of a pair of eyes at about deer height. At the same moment another set of headlights topped the rise coming toward her in the opposite lane.

Instinct took over as she wrenched the wheel to the right, and the truck veered off the pavement. She slammed on the brakes, but not soon enough to stop the truck's forward momentum. With a sense of inevitability, she felt the tires sink into the mud at the edge of the road.

She sat there gasping for breath as the deer she'd missed bounded across the beam of her headlights and off into the darkness. "You're welcome! Send somebody back here with a tow truck, okay?" She'd killed the motor with that stunt, so she started it again and put the truck in Reverse.

As she'd expected, the tires spun uselessly in the mud. Growing up around construction workers, she'd learned an entire vocabulary of swearwords. She used them all as she pounded on the steering wheel in frustration.

Getting stuck in the mud wasn't the end of the world. She had a phone and could call for help…except she wasn't exactly dressed for a tow. Why in hell had she thought that was such a terrific idea?

She had a couple of friends with trucks, but they'd left town for the weekend. That meant calling in the professionals. Maybe they wouldn't notice how she was dressed. Yeah, right.

Before she could dig out her phone, someone knocked on her window. She jerked against the shoulder harness so hard she'd probably left a bruise, which wouldn't matter if she was about to be robbed, killed and left in a shallow grave.

Holding her breath, she turned toward the window. Damon. Damon? She lowered the window.

"Are you okay?" He sounded worried.

She appreciated that more than she could say. "I'm fine. Disgusted, but fine."

"She's fine!" Damon called out.

Cade's voice came through the darkness. "Good to

know. I won't call anybody, then. I can haul her out."
He started backing his truck into position.

So she was saved, sort of. "What are you and Cade
doing here?"

"He was giving me a ride to your house on his way
to Lexi's." He shoved back his old straw cowboy hat.
"What are *you* doing here? I thought we had a date."

"We did! We do! But I realized you didn't have any
way to get to my house, so I decided to drive out here
and surprise you."

"You surprised me, all right. Cade's pretty damned
surprised, too. But I'm glad you're okay and you didn't
hit that deer."

"You and me both." If only she'd stayed put, damn it.
She should have figured out that Cade would be coming into town to see Lexi and could give Damon a ride.

A chain clanked and Damon glanced behind him before turning to her again. "Listen, how about you climb
out and I'll take the wheel?"

"I'd rather not."

"Come on, Phil. I know you're extremely capable,
but you just had a bad scare. It's probably better if you
let me drive."

She leaned closer to him. Sound carried and she
didn't want Cade to hear this. "I can't get out," she
said in an undertone.

"Why not? Did you jam your knee or something?"

"No. I'm wearing a thin silk caftan and I don't have
anything on underneath it. I'm not sure if the material
is see-through. I never tested it."

His eyes widened and he swallowed. "Okay. You
stay right there. Leave the window down so we can
communicate."

"I will."

"*Nothing* underneath?"

"That was part of the surprise."

He took a deep breath. "Lady, you certainly know how to plan a surprise."

"Getting stuck in the mud wasn't supposed to be part of it."

He grinned. "No, but it sure makes the evening more interesting."

"Did you think it would be dull?"

His gaze roamed over what he could see of the caftan and his voice dropped to a husky murmur. "Nothing could be dull with you around, Philomena."

And just like that, the entire episode became so worth it.

5

No underwear. *God help him.*

"Damon?" Cade finished hooking the chain to the undercarriage of Phil's truck and stood to face him. "Hey, buddy, she's okay, right? You look a little shell-shocked."

"She's fine." Damon scrubbed a hand over his face in an attempt to get the image of her naked body out of his head so he could help with the rescue operation.

"I was going to suggest you take the wheel, but you look pretty shook up."

"She wants to do it."

"Okay, then. You stand here and let me know when I've got her clear."

"Sure." Damon wasn't about to explain the situation. If Phil had planned to visit his cabin in a caftan and nothing else, he was the only one who needed to know.

Thinking about it would be a bad idea right now, though. He needed to concentrate on getting her out of the mud so they could move on to…other activities. And he couldn't think about those, either.

Truck tires and mud. That was all that should occupy his mind. Except he'd always thought mud was kind of sexy. Some exclusive spas in California encouraged clients to roll around in the stuff. Doing it alone had no appeal, but if he could roll in the mud with a naked Philomena Turner...

"Damon! Is she out yet?"

With a guilty start, he realized the chain was taut, and Cade's truck was straining, but there wasn't much progress. "Give it more gas!"

Phil must have thought he was talking to her because she gunned the motor. The tires spun and in two seconds he was coated with mud. Or at least, the front of him was.

"Hold it!" He staggered back and pulled his bandanna from his hip pocket. Taking off his hat, which miraculously hadn't caught much of the stuff, he wiped his face as he approached the driver's side of Phil's truck. Mud wasn't so damned sexy, after all.

She sucked in a breath. "You meant that for Cade. Oh, God, I'm sorry."

"I should've said his name. My mistake. And I shouldn't have been so close."

"But if I'd used my head, I would have realized you were talking to him and not me. Now you're covered in mud."

He smiled. "I'll wash."

"I'll clean you up when we get to my house. I promise."

"Are you saying you'll attend to it personally?" The mud itself might not be sexy, but getting rid of it could be.

"Absolutely." She sounded a little out of breath. "It's the least I can do."

"You guys finished with your gab fest?" Cade sounded as if he'd run out of patience.

Damon wasn't surprised. While he was standing here mesmerized by the thought of Phil naked under that silk number, Cade only cared about hauling Phil's truck out of this ditch so he could get on over to see Lexi. "We're ready when you are!"

"Then here goes!" Cade gradually bore down on the gas pedal and his truck inched forward, dragging Phil's out of the mud with a giant sucking sound. All four tires were now on the pavement, although the truck would need a wash as much as Damon did.

"She's clear!" Damon called out.

"What a pain for you guys." Phil sighed.

Damon's chest tightened in sympathy. This episode had embarrassed her. He wanted his bold, confident Philomena back. "Just sit tight and wait for me. After I help Cade stow the chain I'll be back. Do you have a blanket for the seat? I don't want to get it all muddy."

"I have one."

"Great. See you in a minute." He jogged to the back of the truck where Cade was already unhooking the chain.

Cade glanced up and started to laugh. "I had a feeling that's what had happened when you yelled."

"She thought I was talking to her when I called for more gas."

"Easy mistake to make."

"Partly my fault." He helped Cade stow the chain in the back of his pickup. "Thanks for pulling her out, bro."

"You're welcome, but I would have done it for anyone who ran into a ditch trying to avoid a deer." He gazed at Damon. "Was she coming to pay you a visit?"

"Yeah."

"But why? I thought she was expecting you at her place."

Damon explained Phil's decision, and Cade whistled.

"Damn. You've known her what, a little over twenty-four hours? That's fast work, even for a guy like you."

"I know. But we emailed for a couple of weeks before I showed up. We got to know each other."

"But you thought she was a man named Phil, not a woman named Philomena, so I don't think all those emails count."

"Sure they do. They might even count double."

Cade studied him without saying anything.

That made Damon figure he had more explaining to do. "We talked about the job. I never talk to a woman about the job. Do you see what I'm saying?"

"I'm beginning to, but I'm a little confused. According to what you said before, this is supposed to be all about sex. What you're describing to me is sort of like… like bonding. Like what goes on between Lexi and me."

"No, no. It's not *that* deep. I just like her. We like each other. We're not even close to your and Lexi's territory." The idea that Cade thought he might be gave him a moment of panic.

"Look, if you're developing feelings for her, just say so."

"Nope, not in the way you're talking about. Like I said, we're on the same page about my leaving next week."

Cade glanced at him and smiled. "Make sure you shower off before you join her on that page, or in that bed, or whatever is the next step for you two. Are you going on to the cabin or back to her house?"

"Her house. I don't know what kind of bed she has, but it's gotta be larger than my bunk."

Cade laughed. "Guaranteed. Anyway, don't get carried away until you hit the showers."

"It's that bad?"

"Yeah. Mud is not a good look on you, bro. Get rid of it as soon as you can. And now I'm off to see my lady love. I've kept her waiting long enough."

"I understand. Thanks for the ride and the tow. And like I said before, Phil and I can drive in together tomorrow morning. We'll make it early so Rosie won't have a clue."

Cade grinned. "I didn't want to mention this to you before and rain on your parade, but that's so not going to work."

"What's wrong with it?"

"Are you going to make Phil drive you there before breakfast? Because Rosie will be up way before dawn scrambling eggs and making coffee like she always does. If you're not in her kitchen ready to eat it as usual, she'll know something's going on."

Damon thought about that. Asking Phil to get them there an hour early in order to save his reputation didn't seem very gentlemanly. He could wander over and have breakfast in Rosie's kitchen, but what about Phil? Was she supposed to grab a piece of toast before leaving her house while he enjoyed a full ranch breakfast? "I guess sneaking around isn't the best idea." He sighed. "I'll have to talk with Rosie."

"There's really no sneaking around behind her back. She knew about our secret blood-brother ceremony fifteen years ago, and she's even better at detection now than she was then. She has great instincts and eyes in the back of her head."

Damon nodded. "Yep, she does."

"Just tell her and get it over with. If she asks me for my opinion, I'll support your decision to keep your life the way you want it. Maybe if she hears it from both of us, she'll adjust her thinking. Anyway, I'm off."

"Thanks again." Damon clasped Cade's hand in their ritual handshake. Then Cade walked back to his truck and Damon turned and headed in the opposite direction.

Phil leaned out the window. "Thanks, Cade!"

"Welcome! Have fun!" He climbed in his truck and drove off.

Damon walked up to the driver's side and gestured toward his muddy clothes. "All things considered, I should probably ride in back."

"Don't be silly. I put a blanket over the seat like you suggested. Go ahead and get in. It'll be fine."

He shook his head. "Okay. Your truck." And he was glad he wouldn't be riding in the back all the way to her house. He might be muddy, and his hands were dirty from handling the chain, so he couldn't touch her, but at least he could check out this silk outfit of hers.

When he opened the passenger door the dome light came on and he got his first good look at her. His breath caught. Her hair was loose around her shoulders. The blue and green swirling pattern of the silk brought out some subtle shading in her eyes that he hadn't noticed before. They weren't just blue. They were a mixture of blue, green and turquoise.

His attention moved to where the shoulder harness was strapped diagonally across her chest, which pulled the material tight. Maybe it wasn't transparent, but it was damned close.

"Pretty stupid, huh? Driving around with practically nothing on. I won't be doing that again soon."

He swallowed. "Too bad." He could stand here forever watching the silk shift with each breath she took.

As the silence stretched between them, the rhythm of her breathing changed. Her nipples, which had only slightly dented the material before, became clearly outlined. "We...we should go."

He met her gaze and found the same hunger there that was creating a heavy ache in his groin. "The cabin's closer." And he wouldn't have to worry about getting mud all over her house.

She hesitated. "You're right." Then her eyebrows arched. "Getting in?"

He didn't have to be asked twice. But as he sat on the blanket she'd spread over the seat, something on the floor crunched under his boot. "Uh-oh. What did I just squash?"

"Condoms."

"You're kidding."

"No. Buckle up."

He reached down and picked up the mangled box before he fastened his seat belt. "You weren't kidding."

"Nope." She pulled out onto the deserted road.

Holding the box, he looked over at her. "You didn't trust me to have any?" That bothered him more than he would have expected it to.

"I didn't know if you would or not."

"You didn't? After all the emails where we talked about attention to detail?"

"That was construction. This is—"

"No different. I'm a detail-oriented guy, whether I'm talking about building a house or going to bed with a woman. I wouldn't have shown up at your house without these. I'd pull mine out of my pocket to prove it except my pocket's muddy."

"I believe you have them. I should have known you wouldn't forget something that important." She glanced at him. "I insulted you, didn't I?"

"I just thought you knew me better than that."

"I guess I have trouble believing I've found somebody so much like me. I brought them because I'm a detail-oriented woman."

He took a deep breath. "Right. I know that about you. This box shouldn't surprise me at all." He was still turning her other comment over in his mind—that they were very much alike.

He'd thought so, too, until he'd laid eyes on her and decided they couldn't be as alike as he'd thought because…because she was a woman? Whoops. Not cool. He didn't like admitting Rosie might be right about his attitude.

Maybe they were alike in the way they thought and the way they worked a job. But holding this box of condoms emphasized an important difference, one he planned to take full advantage of once he'd ditched the muddy clothes. He might not be used to working side by side with a woman, but he was very familiar with being in bed with one.

Too bad about the bunk situation, but driving all the way back to her house would have been torture, at least for him. She'd agreed to the alternate plan so quickly that she'd probably concluded the same thing. Once again, they thought alike.

Thank God they were almost there. "You'll want to take the back road around to the cabins," he said.

"I'd already planned on that."

"Did I just insult *you*?"

"Not really. You're the one who's afraid of getting in hot water over this, so naturally you're the one who's the most worried about someone seeing my truck here tonight."

"About that. I've decided to talk to Rosie first thing in the morning. She'll find out about us, so I might as well level with her."

"If she gives you a hard time, you're welcome to send her to me."

"Cade said he'd back me up, too. Maybe at last she'll get the picture that I'm not interested in getting married."

"And that's your right."

He looked over at her. "How about you? You planning to settle down with someone?"

"Eventually, if the right guy comes along."

"He'd have to be really special."

She smiled. "Thanks."

"No, I mean it. You're amazing. It'll take a hell of a guy to be worthy of you."

"That's nice of you to say. At the very least, he can't be threatened by the fact that I can operate power tools better than he can."

"Like I said, no average Joe for you." They'd reached the edge of the meadow. "Can you pull around by the bathhouse? My shirt got the worst of it and I'd rather take that off in there. I can also wash the stink of metal off my hands."

"Maybe I like a metallic scent on a man."

"Do you?"

"I don't know." She pulled up next to the bathhouse and parked. "I just don't want you to take too long getting neat and clean."

His body responded with a rush of heat. "Then come in with me. That should hurry me along."

They met at the front of the truck and walked toward the bathhouse. Ordinarily at this point he would have held her hand, but he had mud all down his sleeve, and he didn't want to ruin that sexy silk.

Her feet made slapping sounds as she walked.

"Are you wearing flip-flops?"

"Boots didn't seem to go with the outfit."

He laughed. "Guess not. I like the way it swirls around you. What did you call it again?"

"A caftan. It's a one-size-fits-all that just goes over your head."

That's how it would come off, too. His cock thickened. He thought about the condoms in his pocket. No, that wouldn't be an elegant way to begin, in a utilitarian bathhouse, for God's sake. Shame on him for even thinking it.

A dusk-to-dawn light illuminated the entrance and filtered into the interior, but if he wanted any more light, he'd have to turn on an overhead. He couldn't imagine anything less romantic, and besides, he didn't need to see very well to take off his muddy shirt and wash his hands.

He stepped into the semidarkness and she followed him in. He'd never been in here with a woman before. It felt more illicit than he'd thought it would, especially when he started unfastening the snaps on the cuffs of his shirt.

Her breathing picked up. "This feels sort of risqué, being in a public bathroom with a guy."

He was startled that she'd thought the same thing he had. Apparently, they *were* very much alike. "I won't be long." He popped open the snaps running down the front of his shirt and took it off. Some of the mud had dried and it flaked off onto the floor, but he'd clean that up in the morning.

"Take your time." Her voice had a husky quality.

He was learning to cherish that huskiness. It meant she was thinking about sex. Excellent topic. He rolled up his shirt and used it to brush off dried mud from his jeans. "Stand back. I don't want to flick dried mud on you."

"No worries. Feeling better?"

"Much. My jeans didn't get hit as hard as the shirt. Once I wash my face and hands, I'll be fairly mud-free except for my boots."

"Well done." Her comment was low and sultry.

He sure did love listening to her when she sounded like that. He'd like it even more when they were both naked in his bunk. "We might as well leave the truck down here and walk back to the cabin."

"Fine with me."

He tucked the shirt on the shelf running across the row of sinks. Then he laid his hat on top of the shirt. He'd retrieve them in the morning, too. Nobody came down here except him, anyway.

His image in the closest mirror above the sink was shadowy. That was okay. He could still wash his hands and face. In the process he'd make sure he didn't have mud in his hair.

"Almost done." As he soaped and rinsed his hands

and face, he realized he didn't have anything to dry with. "Could you hand me that towel by the shower, please?"

"Sure thing, cowboy."

He felt a brush of silk against his bare back, and then she reached around his waist to hand him the towel. Nice move. "Thanks." As he dried his face, she reached in with her other hand and spread her palms over his abs.

"Mmm." She nestled against him from behind. "Very nice."

The unexpected caress sent his blood straight to his cock, which pushed against his fly. He dropped the towel into the sink. "Phil…"

"What?"

"I hope you know what you're doing."

"I know exactly what I'm doing." She rubbed her silk-covered breasts against his back. "Do you?"

"I think…you're seducing me."

"Bingo." She reached for his belt buckle.

"Here?"

"For starters." She had his buckle undone in no time.

He braced his hands against the sink and let her complete the job. Only a fool would stop a woman intent on getting her hands inside his… Ah, yes. Heaven was having Phil wrap her fingers around his throbbing cock.

As she fondled him, she ran her tongue along his backbone. Naturally, that made him think of what else she could do with her tongue, but he wasn't going to ask. He *couldn't* ask. He was having trouble breathing, let alone talking.

She didn't seem to have that problem. "I think you

need to turn around." And she withdrew those magic hands.

He turned. Cupping her face, he kissed her with an intensity that might have worried him if he'd thought about it. But he was way beyond thinking. He craved the feel of her mouth against his. He needed to thrust his tongue deep inside and hear her moan.

And oh, did she moan. She also continued her sweet assault, reaching inside his briefs to stroke and squeeze until he gasped and broke away from the kiss. If she kept it up he was going to come, and he didn't want that. Not yet.

"Easy." He struggled to get the words out. "Or this will be over too soon."

Her soft chuckle seemed especially erotic in this setting. "Feeling like a teenager again?" Her thumb nestled against the tender cleft beneath the head of his cock.

"Yes, and you know how they are."

"Ready to walk to the cabin?"

"You're kidding."

"Then maybe we'd better see what's in your pocket."

He wouldn't have chosen this as their first time, but he was out of options. His climax pounded at the door and rattled the windows, wanting to be turned loose. He dug a condom out of his pocket, ripped open the package and rolled it on.

In the time he took to do that, she'd whipped her dress over her head and hung it on the hook where his towel used to be. Then she kicked off her flip-flops. He regretted that he couldn't see her better. He knew she would be magnificent.

But the moment was upon them. She clutched his

shoulders as he braced himself against the sink, cupped her smooth bottom and lifted her up.

She propped her feet on that same sink, her thighs tight around his waist. "I hope your plumbing is sturdy."

"It is." And with that he lowered her onto his rigid penis. He'd never been this hard or this desperate for release. But as she sank down, enveloping his urgency with heat and urgency of her own, he fought his natural instinct to push upward and let go.

Instead he stopped moving and just stood there while he regained command of himself. That wasn't an easy task, with heat sizzling through his veins and every muscle in his body screaming for release.

She leaned back and gazed at him, although she couldn't possibly see much. "Come if you need to."

"Oh, I need to, but I won't. Not yet. Do you need to?"

"Yes."

"Then that's what will happen. Work with me, Philomena."

Her response was part laughter and part moan as she used the sink and his shoulders as leverage. He steadied her as she moved up and down, massaging his aching bad boy with every stroke. It was torture, but the sweetest torture he could imagine.

Somehow he held back until she came, arching against him and clenching her jaw against the cries that carried far too readily in the cool mountain air. The firm grip of her climax pushed him past his limit and he surged upward, claiming his reward. He swallowed a groan of pleasure so great that he wanted to shout it to the world.

As they trembled in the aftermath of their first shared climax, he vowed that very soon he'd find a place and a time where they could make all the joyful noise they wanted. Something this good deserved to be celebrated.

Then a little voice inside his head whispered that something this good was worth hanging on to. But he refused to listen.

6

THE NIGHT WASN'T turning out anything like Phil had anticipated, but she couldn't complain. She'd had amazing sex in a dark bathhouse, of all places. And a very short time after that, she found herself stretched out on Damon's narrow bunk. Bathed in the glow of a small desk lamp, she trembled in anticipation as he nibbled and kissed every inch of her.

He was exceptionally good at that. His attention to detail on the construction site carried over into his lovemaking, and she was the happy recipient of his thoroughness. He found the sensitive spot on the inside of her elbow, and taught her that even the spaces between her fingers were erogenous zones.

She had a pretty fair idea what his ultimate plan was for this kiss-fest, but she didn't know how he'd accomplish it in such cramped quarters. No way could he prop himself between her thighs and be comfortable. Most of him would be hanging off the end of the bunk.

As it turned out, he had an alternate plan. Dropping to his knees beside the bed, he settled her crossways on the mattress with her feet on the floor. They didn't stay on the floor for long, though. Soon he draped her legs over his broad shoulders, and she was enjoying the agility of his nimble tongue in her most erogenous of all zones.

How she wanted to make noise! But she didn't dare. The cabin's windows were open to catch the breeze, and the ranch house windows undoubtedly would be open, too. So as Damon provided one shattering climax, and then another, she grabbed his pillow and smothered her cries.

While she was still quivering from that second whirl-wind experience, he gently guided her back onto the bed, rolled on another condom and slid easily into her drenched channel. Dazed with pleasure, she looked into the warmth of his gray eyes.

"Tell me if you're getting tired." He began a slow, easy rhythm.

"Not yet." She felt decadent, sensual and incredibly relaxed. But not tired. The wonder of making love to this man might never wear off. He was inventive and yet patient, forceful and yet considerate. She'd never known anyone like him.

"Before I forget." He continued his lazy rocking motion. "I'd like a ride to your place after the barbecue tomorrow night."

That made her smile. "You don't want to hang out here afterward?"

"Don't get me wrong. I love this." He paused and cinched himself in tight. "I really love it." He leaned down and dropped a soft kiss on her mouth. "But I'm guessing your bed is larger."

"A king."

He nibbled on her lower lip. "We could have a lot of fun in a king-size bed, Philomena."

"We could." And the thought of that tightened a coil of excitement deep within her. She imagined him stretched out on her blue-patterned sheets, his cock firm and waiting for her as she straddled him. She didn't dare try that here. She'd hit her head on the top bunk.

But in her bed, the one no man had ever enjoyed, she could frolic and play with this gorgeous cowboy. "We could make noise," she murmured. "I don't have any close neighbors."

"Good. I want that." He shifted his angle and increased the pace. "I want to hear you when you come."

"I want to hear you, too."

"Oh, you will." His lazy motion was gone. He bore down, driving into her with swift, sure thrusts. "Because you make me want to make noise. Your hot body drives me crazy, and all I want is to keep pumping into you while I watch your pupils get darker and darker, until you come apart, like *now*."

Right on cue, she erupted in a glorious climax. He covered her mouth with his, muffling her cries as he pushed deep. Then it was his turn. She swallowed his heavy groan as her body welcomed the rhythmic pulse of his orgasm.

As he grew still, he lifted his head to gaze into her eyes. "You're incredible."

"No, *you're* incredible."

He smiled. "You inspire me, Philomena." He settled gently against her and rested his head on the pillow next to hers. His breath was warm against her ear. "I'll move in a minute, but I just want to stay here for a little longer. You feel so good."

"So do you." Joy. That was the only word to describe the emotion flooding through her as she lay, sweaty and satisfied, beneath him. She didn't feel squashed, which meant he must be keeping his weight on his arms. He deserved a whole bunch of gold stars.

She was imagining what fun it would be to draw stars on his muscled body with a gold pen when she drifted off to sleep. Sometime later she woke up to discover the light was off and he wasn't in bed with her anymore. But he was here somewhere. She could hear his steady breathing. She sat up. Moonlight coming through the window allowed her to see fairly well as she glanced around.

As she'd expected, he was asleep on the bottom bunk across the room from her. It seemed wrong to be so far from each other after what they'd shared, but they'd never be able to sleep comfortably in one bunk. He didn't quite fit lying there by himself, let alone if she were crammed in beside him.

She had no idea what time it was, but she couldn't stay here until morning. That had been one disadvantage of this plan. She'd have to drive back home to shower and change before showing up ready to work.

A clock wasn't in evidence, so if she wanted to know the time, she'd have to get her phone. Slipping out of bed, she tried to remember what she'd done with her purse. Then she saw it lying by the door where she'd dropped it when Damon had started kissing her.

Her first step made the floor creak, and she paused. She didn't want to wake up her sleeping sweetie, but she needed to find out the time. His breathing hadn't changed, so she took another step, and the floor groaned. Damn! She hadn't noticed this before, but then, she'd been too busy kissing Damon to pay attention to a noisy floor.

"Going somewhere?" He propped himself on his elbow and gazed at her.

"I woke you. I'm so sorry. The floor—"

"Creaks something fierce. I know." He ducked down as he climbed out of the lower bunk. "When I'm more awake and coordinated, I can play a tune on it."

"That's funny." But she didn't care about the floor anymore. Her eyes had adjusted to the dim light, which allowed her to drink in the sight of a naked Damon walking toward her. Earlier she'd been too distracted by all the kissing and fondling to fully appreciate his masculine beauty.

He'd be an artist's dream with his broad shoulders, muscular chest and lean hips. His abs gave new meaning to the term *washboard*, and his powerful thigh muscles flexed with each step. She also couldn't help noticing the change that had taken place since he first left the bunk. His magnificent cock was now proudly erect. Her pulse quickened.

"I'm glad the floor woke me up." His gaze swept over her. "You look great in moonlight."

"You, too." Her body moistened. The sweet ache of desire teased her with the possibility of one more orgasm. Just one. Then she'd go home.

"Were you going to leave without telling me?"

She caught a tiny note of panic in his voice and realized it would have bothered him if she had. "I thought I should let you sleep. I need to drive home so I can dress for work. But I don't know what time it is, so I was going to check my phone."

"It's two-fifteen."

"How do you know?"

He held up his phone with the screen facing her.

"Oh." She hadn't seen it nestled in his big hand, probably because she'd been focused on something else entirely.

"I set the alarm for three-thirty, figuring that would give you plenty of time to make the round trip plus grab a shower and some breakfast."

She was beginning to understand exactly how conscientious this man was. And she'd thought he might forget condoms. She'd done him a disservice. "You weren't going to let me oversleep."

"I knew you wouldn't like that."

"No. No, I wouldn't. But I woke up early, so I've messed with your very considerate plan. Do you...want to go back to sleep?"

He chuckled. "Do I look like I want to go back to sleep?"

"Not exactly."

"Are you sleepy?"

If she said yes, he'd encourage her to go back to bed and ignore his body's reaction to her. She knew that about him, now. But as she gazed at the evidence that he was definitely *not* sleepy, her body began to hum. "Not anymore."

"Any suggestion as to how we might pass the time until you have to leave? Because if you can't think of anything, I might have a few ideas."

She had an idea, all right. She had a sudden urge to be completely in charge of this gorgeous, complicated man. "How about if you go sit in that desk chair over there?"

"Okay." He started toward it.

"Oh, wait. Where are the condoms?"

He held out his other hand, palm up. A condom packet rested in the middle of it.

"What are you, an amateur magician?"

"Just detail oriented. I set the alarm in case we both kept sleeping, and I put a condom by my pillow in case we didn't."

"Then I'll just take that little item." She plucked it from his hand. "You seem to have thought of everything."

"Apparently not." He walked over to the armless chair. "I never envisioned sitting bare-assed on this faux-leather seat." He sat down and rolled himself toward her. "What now?"

"I didn't think about the fact it rolls." She tore open the condom packet as she approached. "Can you hold it still?"

"I don't know. How excited am I liable to get?"

"Let's try this and see." Leaning over him, she started rolling the condom on.

He sucked in a breath. "You'd think I could take that without wanting to come."

"You'd think I could do it without shaking." She finished the job and cupped his face with both hands. "You'd think I wouldn't want you again so soon. And so much I can't see straight." She gave him an open-mouthed kiss with lots of tongue.

He groaned and grabbed her around the waist. He must have figured out her idea, because he started guiding her hips and scooting the chair between her thighs.

She lifted her mouth from his. "Let me do it."

"Does that matter?"

"Yes. Let go."

He slid both hands up her rib cage and cradled her breasts. "Can I hold you here?"

"Gently."

His voice was thick with desire. "I'm always gentle."

"Yeah." She sank back into their hot, wet kiss. He really might be a magician. He certainly had magic hands. The sensuous way he squeezed and massaged her breasts almost made her forget her original idea, especially with the way he sucked on her tongue.

Then he rolled the chair just enough that the tip of his penis brushed her moist cleft and sent a sharp zing of awareness to every nerve in her body. Straddling his hips, she braced her hands on his shoulders and lowered herself just enough to enclose that sensitive tip.

He moaned.

She eased down a little more, and his whole body quivered.

So did hers. She was teasing herself as much as she was teasing him.

And it was delicious, so delicious that she wanted to draw it out. She'd make them both a little crazy before she was finished. She rose up a fraction and slid back to where she'd been before.

He groaned this time, a sound that seemed to come from the depths of that impressive chest. He pulled back from her kiss, and his voice was strained. "More."

"Soon." Her heart beat a rapid tattoo as she lifted her hips again and slipped back down, taking him in a little more this time, but not much. Not as far as he would want.

His breathing roughened. "Phil..."

"Let's test our limits." She moved slowly back up and

just as slowly back down. She was so wet, so ready to come, but she wouldn't. Not yet.

"My cock feels like a stick of dynamite."

Reaching down, she wrapped her fingers around the base of it.

He responded with a sharp gasp.

"You're right." She squeezed him and let go. "It does." And suddenly she wanted it, all of it. She couldn't hold back any longer. Dragging in a shaky breath, she pushed down and took every glorious inch of him.

"Thank you!"

"Shh. People are asleep." She kissed him again, loving the supple feel of his mouth and the erotic stroke of his tongue. Kissing Damon felt almost as good as having his cock buried deep inside her. Almost.

But she couldn't kiss him and do what she'd intended, so reluctantly she pulled back. "You need to let go of me and let me do this."

"I could help."

"I want to do it."

"What should I hold on to?"

"The chair. Keep the chair steady." And with that, she began to move, faster, and faster yet. Her bottom slapped against his thighs, and he groaned through clenched teeth.

But the chair didn't move. He kept it rock-solid as she rode him for all she was worth until she came in a blaze of glory and he followed right after her. She slumped against him, panting, with her feet resting lightly on the floor.

At least they were on the floor until he reached down and grabbed her behind the knees. "Hang on, Philomena." And he gave the chair a push, and then another, and pretty soon they were scooting around the room, laughing like kids on a carnival ride as the floor creaked merrily underneath them.

At last he brought the chair to a stop and lowered her feet to the floor. His grin flashed in the moonlit room. "Bet you've never done that before."

"Bet you never have, either."

"Nope, that's a first. But hey, if you're gonna have sex on a rolling chair, it seems a shame not to do some rolling to commemorate the moment, especially if you're on a floor that talks back. By the way, that's why I wanted a concrete slab for the new one."

"I see." She gazed up at him. "Are you sure we should go to my house tomorrow night? It could be dull after this experience."

"Technically it's tonight, since it's now the Fourth, but yes, we should. This is a small cabin with small beds. I think we've squeezed about all the fun out of it that we can. I'm ready for the big time."

"So it's officially the Fourth of July." She would remember this particular one for a long, long time.

"And thanks to you waking up early, we've already had fireworks."

"So we have." She ran a fingertip over his full lower lip. "Thanks for going along with my teasing."

He nipped at her finger. "I thought you were going to kill me."

"But you were a good sport."

"You know what? It was fantastic. You've given me some ideas for next time."

"Can't wait." She imagined how he'd arrange payback and was ready to start immediately.

His expression grew serious. "But before we get to

have this kind of fun again, we have to work together on that cabin and keep our hands to ourselves. That'll be a challenge for me."

"For me, too."

"Can we do it?"

"We have to." She sighed. "And speaking of that, I'd better drive home." She kissed him once more before slowly standing and moving away from the chair. Her caftan lay in a heap next to her purse, and she walked across the creaky floor to pick it up.

Behind her, the rustle of a tissue box indicated he was taking care of the condom. "I hope your silk outfit is okay."

"It'll be fine." And if it wasn't, she didn't care. Sacrificing her caftan for this eventful night with Damon was a no-brainer. It wasn't torn, so it would keep her from getting arrested on the way home. She located her flip-flops and wiggled her feet into them. "I'm ready."

"Hang on. I'll walk you to your truck."

"That's—" She was about to say it wasn't necessary, but she changed her mind. "That's very nice of you." Seeing her to her truck would be important to him. Come to think of it, she'd like for him to do that.

They might have an understanding about how this liaison would end, but at heart he was a cowboy, and cowboys had a code of chivalry. She'd grown up around men who had that same code. She'd been the one who'd insisted they should treat her like one of the guys. Left to themselves, they would have put her on a pedestal.

Maybe that was part of the problem with Damon. His instinct was to put women on a pedestal, even if they knew how to operate both a forklift and a compressor. Dealing with someone like her, who was both a competent coworker on the site and a passionate woman in his bed, must be straining his brain.

She had no such problem. For her, he was the perfect combination—a guy she could count on while they worked together and a lover who knew how to please her better than any man she'd run across. She didn't want to think about that too much, though. If he was perfect, then she'd miss him all the more when he was gone. And he would go. He'd told her so, and so far, he'd been a man of his word.

7

DAMON HAD TROUBLE letting Phil leave, and he recognized that as a danger sign. Because she was so different from any woman he'd known, she made him think of things that he hadn't allowed himself to think about before.

For example, she intended to get married and have kids. Other women he'd dated had announced the same thing and he'd accepted that reality, no problem. But he found himself thinking about the lucky bastard Phil would end up with and the cute kids she'd have with some guy who wouldn't be worthy of her.

He already knew her potential husband wouldn't be good enough. She was special, and he didn't like the odds of her discovering a perfect match in Sheridan. The pool was too small. She might settle for someone who didn't quite measure up, and he hated that idea.

Those were the kind of nonproductive thoughts running through his head as he kept her standing beside her truck for way too long while they kissed and cuddled and talked about how they'd get through the next few hours until they could be alone. Prolonging goodbyes wasn't his normal style, and he was well aware of it. If he'd faced the situation logically, he'd have realized that in seventeen or eighteen hours, they'd be rolling around in her king-size bed. That wasn't very far away.

Oh, yes, it was. The minute her truck pulled out, he began to ache for her. Not good. Cade's words came back to him. *Sounds like bonding...if you're developing feelings for her, just say so.*

Well, of course he had feelings for her. She was a terrific woman. He'd be an idiot not to recognize that and feel happy that she'd decided to spend time with him. That didn't mean he was ready to change his whole life, a life that suited him right down to the ground.

Because he was too restless to go back to sleep, he walked into the bathhouse, flipped on a light and found the broom and dustpan. First he swept the floor. Then he took his shirt and hat outside to shake off the rest of the dried mud. All the while he replayed the great time he'd had with Phil. Damn, she'd been sexy when she'd come up behind him and put her hands on his bare chest.

He would always remember their wild sex in the bathhouse. He'd never in a million years have expected that such a utilitarian space would be where he'd give Philomena Turner an orgasm for the first time. That particular sink, the second from the right, would forever remind him of her.

Whoa. Was he storing memories of this love affair? He never did that. Soon after moving to California he'd been introduced to the concept of Zen, living in the moment, and he'd applied it immediately to his life— including his sex life. When he was with a lady, he was totally with her. Once they parted ways, he seldom thought of her again.

For whatever reason—because he was back in Wyoming or because Phil was nothing like the women he'd dated in California, he was collecting memories. Another warning sign. If Rosie could read his thoughts, she'd be laughing her head off.

Well, he'd take care of that pronto. He already had a head start on the morning, so he might as well take advantage of it. He'd show up early for breakfast in Rosie's kitchen so he could explain to her why he would never get serious about any woman, especially Philomena Turner.

By four-thirty he'd showered, shaved and dressed in a white T-shirt and jeans. A faint wash of gray rimmed the horizon as he walked up to the ranch house, but the sun wouldn't be up for another hour. He could hear Herb whistling in the barn while he fed the horses.

Normally, Damon would have stopped by to give him a hand, but he wanted a chance to talk with Rosie alone. A light shone from the kitchen window, which meant Rosie was up and working on breakfast as she'd done for all the years he'd known her.

Herb didn't have a talent for cooking, but he'd always helped clean up the kitchen after the meal. The boys had been assigned to barn duty, helping Rosie cook or clean up. Chores had been rotated to give everyone a shot at every job, but if someone turned out to be especially good at something, he usually got to do it more often. Cleanup had been Damon's specialty. Still was.

Rosie had on old jeans and a plaid shirt that had seen better days—her typical uniform when she would spend the day cooking and cleaning for a party. She had biscuits in the oven, but she hadn't started on the rest of the meal or made the coffee.

She put a large cast-iron skillet on a back burner and gave him a quick smile. "You're up bright and early. Excited about the party?"

"Yes, ma'am." As a kid living here, he'd been all about the parties. When you were thirteen and you'd never had one, you tended to get excited about the prospect of a celebration. He'd outgrown that, mostly, but to Rosie, he'd always be the boy who loved parties.

And he was looking forward to it, even if it meant he wouldn't get to be alone with Phil until late. Lexi's parents, two people he liked a lot, would be there, along with various other friends Herb and Rosie had made over the years. Plus at least two other guys who'd lived here as foster kids had promised to come. It would be great to see them again and find out how they were doing.

He was especially interested in talking with Ty Slater who had a successful law practice in Cheyenne. Ty was handling the legal aspects of the Kickstarter program, and Damon wanted to know all the particulars. So much depended on the success of Thunder Mountain Academy.

He crossed to the counter. "Want me to start the coffee?"

"That would be wonderful." She took a package of bacon out of the refrigerator and began laying strips of it in the skillet. "Seems like old times, having you in the kitchen helping out."

He dumped beans into an electric grinder. "I know. I've missed it." He hadn't meant to say that. Sure as the world she'd latch on to a statement like that. He turned on the coffee grinder partly to cut off her inevitable comment.

Of course that didn't work. She folded her arms and waited until the high-pitched whining stopped. Her determined blue gaze settled on him. "You could always move back here. I'm sure you could find houses to flip in Sheridan."

"Not in the volume I have in Southern California." He smiled to soften his response. "A highly populated area is better for what I do." He dumped the ground coffee into the basket.

"Yes, but our cost of living is less, and if you're not happy, then—"

"I *am* happy." He went to the sink and filled the carafe with water. "I love my job. In fact, that's something I wanted to talk to you about."

"Okay." The bacon sizzled in the pan, and she turned her attention to it, flipping it over with a long-handled fork. "Could you please get a carton of eggs out of the fridge? I forgot. My mind's on a million different things this morning."

"I'm sure it is." He hadn't thought about her being in party mode this morning. It might not be the best time for this little talk, but tomorrow would be too late. It was now or never.

He set down the carafe and opened the refrigerator. It was packed with the makings for party food, which was a sight that always gave him a lift. He handed her the eggs and went back to pour the water into the coffeemaker and turn it on. "I don't think I ever explained why I love flipping houses."

"I know you like fixing them up." She began cracking the eggs into a bowl.

"I don't just like it. I love it. A house is usually in terrible shape when I move in, but by the time I move out, it shines. I can't wait to show it off. When someone buys it and I hand them the keys, it's a real rush."

Rosie glanced up as she continued to beat the eggs with a wire whisk. "I can understand that. We have trashed houses in Wyoming, too, you know."

"Not enough of them within driving distance to feed my habit. But that's not the point I want to make. Moving into a house allows me to work on it whenever I feel like it, which suits me. When I'm constantly there, I think of ways to fix it that might not occur to me otherwise. I've found a perfect method."

"I see." She turned back to the stove. "How about monitoring the bacon while I scramble the eggs?"

"I'd be glad to." He joined her at the stove.

"This really is like old times."

"And they were good times. I promise to visit more often." He flipped the bacon and turned down the heat. "But back to what I was saying. Do you understand how satisfied I am with my job?"

"I do, but it would be a hell of a life for a family."

"That's why I don't plan on having one."

"But—"

"Mom, not everyone wants to get married and have kids. I like my life as it is."

She stirred the eggs. "You're saying all this because of Philomena, aren't you?"

"Yes, ma'am. I like her. I like her a lot."

"So I figured when you hitched a ride into town with Cade last night."

And he thought they'd been so discreet. Ha.

"I knew you weren't planning to hang out at Lexi's with him," she continued. "But his truck isn't back yet. How did you get home?"

He sighed. "I'd rather not go into detail, but let's just say the evening didn't work out quite the way I expected. The bottom line is that tonight after the barbecue, Phil's giving me a ride to her house. I wanted you to know in advance."

Herb walked into the kitchen. "You're going over to Phil's tonight? That's fast work, son."

"Oh, he's a fast worker, all right." Rosie didn't sound happy. "Has Phil heard this little speech of yours about how your working style doesn't leave room for a wife and family?"

"Yes, and she's fine with it."

"I see." Rosie glanced at Herb. "Get us some plates, please, honey. The food's done even if this discussion isn't."

Herb pulled plates and coffee mugs out of the cupboard and shortly they were seated at the kitchen table where Rosie could skewer Damon with one of her disapproving stares. "Philomena is a nice girl."

"Yes, she is." He met her gaze. "I'm sure that's why you set me up with her."

Rosie had the good grace to blush. "She's perfect for you, Damon. I guarantee she understands your dedication to your work. She's the same way."

"She is. I respect her abilities more than I can say. And you were right about one thing."

"*One* thing?" Rosie's expression darkened.

"I'm sure you didn't mean it like that, did you, son?" Herb gave him a sympathetic glance.

"No. You're right about a lot of things, Mom. In this case, you were right that I had a blind spot."

"Which blind spot are we referring to, pray tell? I can think of at least two off the top of my head."

He thought that was a pot-and-kettle situation, but he wisely didn't say so. "I assumed the person who would be helping me was a guy, and I shouldn't have. I won't make that mistake again."

"Better widen your net," Herb said. "Include everybody—firefighters, jet pilots, truck drivers, you name it."

"I will." Damon looked at Rosie. "I appreciate the nudge. I had some old-fashioned thinking going on."

"That's something, at least." She shook her head. "But I don't know about this other business. I'd better talk with Philomena. You say she's fine with some fly-by-night affair, but I want to make sure she's—"

"I'm telling you, she accepts this about me. It's the way I've been with ladies ever since I hit puberty, so I don't know why it should surprise you. Nothing's changed." If he sounded frustrated, then it was because he *was* becoming extremely frustrated. "I'm not the settling-down type."

"I know, and when you were younger, I didn't worry about it. Lots of boys play the field."

"But I'm a grown man now, and that's still my pattern over in California."

She sighed. "I know that, too, but it's not happening under my nose. And I keep hoping you'll see the light. I thought maybe if you met the perfect woman, which Phil definitely is, you'd realize—"

"Mom." He reached over and put a hand on her arm. "Please try to understand this. My life is great. I have work I love and most of the time I have a woman in my life. Just not the same woman, which is how I like it."

She glanced at him in horror. "Please don't tell me you have a girlfriend in California."

"No! I'm not that kind of guy. Geez. If I had a girl-friend I wouldn't have had—" He caught himself, but his face got warm, which meant he was turning red.

"Sex with Philomena?" Rosie's tone was light, but her blue eyes shot sparks.

This was not the discussion he wanted to have with his foster mother. "I haven't deceived her. I explained how things were right from the beginning, before we ever… Anyway, she's okay with it."

"So you say. I intend to find that out for myself. Now eat your breakfast before it gets cold."

So he did, partly because she'd told him to and he'd been in the habit of following that particular order since he was thirteen. But also, Rosie cooked a damned good breakfast, and he was starving. Lots of sex combined with very little sleep could do that to a person. He devoured more than his share of the biscuits, too.

As was typical with her, Rosie noticed. "Worked up an appetite, did you?"

He glanced over to find her watching him with amusement. Maybe she wasn't quite as mad at him as she'd acted. He swallowed the bite he'd finished chewing. "Yes, ma'am." He was reaching for another biscuit when his phone chimed. "Excuse me." He pulled his phone from his pocket, and when he noticed the time on his screen, he figured the text was from Phil wondering where he was.

Sure enough, she was down at the site. He texted back that he'd be right there. "If you'll excuse me, I need to go." He picked up his mug and plate as he stood. "Thanks for breakfast. It was delicious."

Rosie looked up at him. "Was that Phil?"

"Yes, ma'am."

"Would you please ask her to come up here for a few minutes?"

His reluctance must have been obvious even though he hadn't said a word.

"Do you want to be here when I talk to her? Because that's fine with me. You can call her now and invite her up for a cup of coffee. We'll sit around the kitchen table and have a chat."

Herb pushed back his chair. "You'll have to do that without me. I need to check the automatic watering system in the barn. It's not acting right."

"Just like some people around here," Rosie muttered.

Herb must be using the watering system as an excuse so he could escape. He wasn't good with repairs. Damon decided to ask him later today if he needed help with it.

In the meantime, he'd attempt to derail Rosie's plan. "The thing is, Phil and I have a lot of work to accomplish before the party, so…" He trailed off as Rosie gave him what the boys used to call *the look.* "Okay, I'll go down and send her up here. And to answer your question, I don't have to be present. I already know what she's going to say."

"You do? And how long have you known her?"

"Well, technically, a couple of days, but we wrote all those emails, so I've actually known her longer."

Rosie didn't seem impressed. "She's been handling routine maintenance around here for about four years. I've watched her business grow, and I've watched her grow as a person. I realize now that I might've put her in a no-win situation, and I need to talk to her about it."

"A no-win situation?" He didn't like the sound of that. "How do you figure?"

"I hate to say this and give you a swelled head, but

you're a good-looking man. And you're extremely charming. If you've already lured her into bed, then—"

"I didn't lure her! The attraction is exceedingly mutual!"

"Which would be great if you could see how perfect she is for you. I really thought you would, but I guess I was wrong. I'm worried that she'll get hurt."

"How can she when she's going into it with her eyes wide-open?"

Rosie gazed at him. "Son, I love you to death, but you have a lot to learn about women."

He thought about that as he walked down to the meadow. Was Rosie right? Even though Phil had insisted that a temporary affair was no problem, might it be after all? In other words, Phil could be fooling herself. She might be sacrificing her best interests because the chemistry between them was so strong.

If there was the slightest chance of that, the right choice would be to stay out of Phil's bed for the rest of the time he was in Wyoming. He wasn't sure he was that noble.

8

WHILE PHIL WAITED for Damon, she started uncrating windows, which would go in today if they worked steadily. She'd expected to see him at the site when she'd arrived at five-thirty, so she'd checked his cabin and the bathhouse. Both were tidy, but he wasn't in either place. At last she'd figured he was having breakfast in the ranch house kitchen.

He'd mentioned that he wanted to talk with Rosie, and this would be a good opportunity if he was planning to boldly take off for her house after the barbecue tonight. Thinking Rosie might be giving him a hard time, she'd texted him, in case he'd needed an excuse to get the heck out of there.

His immediate response suggested that might have been the case. In very short order he rounded the corner of the house and started toward the meadow. She resisted the urge to run into his arms in fake slow motion like a movie heroine. Now probably wasn't the time to act goofy.

He was the same gorgeous hunk of manhood she'd left only two hours earlier. His shoulders were just as broad, and his walk just as loose and sexy. But something about his body language told her all was not peachy in his world.

When he was close enough for her to see his expression under the shadow of his straw cowboy hat, she knew that for sure. She went to meet him. "What's wrong?"

"Rosie wants to see you up at the house for a chat."

"Oh, boy. That sounds like a summons."

"It sort of is. I tried to get you out of it, but she insisted."

"That's fine. I'm not surprised she wants to see me. I assume you told her about us."

"Yep."

"Then I'd better go find out what she has to say about it."

"Listen, before you go, I want you to be honest with me. Is it remotely possible you'll be all torn up when I leave next week?"

She looked into those beautiful gray eyes. "Rosie thinks I will, doesn't she?"

"Never mind Rosie. What she thinks doesn't matter. Well, it does, because I love her and she's my mom, but this is between you and me."

She thought about how to answer.

"Don't sugarcoat it, Phil. Is my approach to this affair likely to cause you pain?"

She took a deep breath. "It's possible."

"Shit."

"But I don't care."

"How can you not care? Most people I know try to avoid pain. They don't stick their hand in an open flame or smash their kneecap with a two-by-four because they know it won't be any fun doing that. If my leaving is going to be painful for you, then we need to reconsider whether to go forward."

"Before we make that sacrifice, let's turn things around. Will leaving me cause *you* pain?"

He looked puzzled. "Well, I'm not going to enjoy it, if that's what you mean."

"No, that's not what I mean. Let's say we go ahead with the plan and you spend the next five nights with me. Then you hop on a plane and head back to California. Can you imagine how you'll feel at that point?"

"Sad, because I like being with you and I'll miss you." He smiled. "Probably sexually frustrated after all those nights in your bed. I'll get used to regular sex with you, and suddenly it'll be gone."

"Would you say your feelings will be painful?"

He chuckled. "They could be if thinking about you makes me hard and I'm strapped into an economy-class seat."

"How about here?" She put her hand over his heart.

"Yeah." His voice softened. "I'll be hurting there, too."

"So we'll be in the same boat. You won't be causing me any more pain than you're causing yourself. It's like when I was teasing you on the desk chair. I teased myself at the same time."

He nudged his hat back with his thumb. "You would have to bring that up."

"It's a good analogy."

"And it makes me want to drag you into my cabin and do it all over again."

Her breath hitched. "We can't." But now she wanted that, too. Her whole body vibrated with wanting.

"Stop looking at me that way."

She closed her eyes. "Is that better?"

"Hell, no." And he was there, tugging her close and kissing her hard as he pushed the ridge of his cock against her belly.

She responded by cupping his ass and pulling him in tighter. Moisture and heat gathered between her thighs as he thrust his tongue into her mouth. She moaned, and he shoved his hands in her back pockets, his fingers flexing against the worn denim.

Then he abruptly released her and stepped back, gasping. "This is not good."

When she opened her eyes she saw that his hat had fallen off, his fists were clenched and fire was in his gaze.

"Oh, no, it's very good, cowboy." She gulped for air. "And don't you forget it. I can't speak for you, but I'm willing to accept a sad goodbye when I think of all the pleasure we can find in the next five nights together."

A shudder ran through him. "I said I couldn't resist you. That's truer now than it was then. It'll take all my willpower to work alongside you today without grabbing you, but I'll do it, because the whole time I'll be thinking about what will happen tonight."

She smiled. "I put fresh sheets on the bed."

The heat in his eyes intensified. "I'd hate to see that kind of effort go to waste."

"Exactly."

"You'd better go talk to Rosie. She's riddled with guilt. She thinks she's put you in a no-win situation with me."

"That's not how I look at it. Lots of mutual pleasure feels like win-win to me."

"Are you going to tell her that?"

"Depends. Does she know we've had sex?"

He nodded. "My fault. The conversation got a little out of hand and I slipped up."

Her heart went out to him. "Don't worry about it. She'd have known by tonight, anyway, so it doesn't matter." She paused while she considered how much to say. "Look, I have some idea of how important Rosie is to you."

"She saved my life."

His expression made her long to wrap her arms around him and hang on, not for sexual reasons but for comfort. "And I'm sure you'll always honor that. But…it's still your life. You have the right to choose how to live it."

His voice was gruff with emotion. "Thank you for saying that."

"I'd better go. As you can see, I started uncrating the windows."

"I'll finish that up, but I don't want to start work on the walls again until you're here."

"Why not? I'm sure you could do the whole job alone if you had to. It would just take longer."

"I could, but this is our project now. I want to put the walls up together."

That affected her more than it probably should. She blamed lack of sleep for the way her throat closed up and her eyes misted. "I won't be long." She turned and started for the house. *Our project now.* He was getting invested, whether he realized it or not. So was she, but she recognized the telltale signs. He might be deliberately ignoring them.

Rosie had a fresh pot of coffee brewed when Phil

walked into the kitchen. She could use another cup after getting about three hours of sleep. She accepted the full mug gratefully and sat at the kitchen table as she had so many times when she'd talked with Rosie over the years.

Conversation had always flowed easily between them on a variety of topics. Today, though, the atmosphere was tense. Phil regretted that, but it couldn't be helped.

"So." Rosie cradled her own mug. "I'm afraid my brilliant plan backfired."

"Damon told me about your misgivings, but I don't feel that way."

Rosie sighed, and her gaze was troubled. "I've known you for several years, but I've known Damon longer. He has a way of getting under your skin. I remember how lost I felt when he moved to California. You're such a positive, sunny personality. If I thought that he would somehow mess with that…"

Phil leaned forward. "If you're imagining some scenario where I hide in my house, stop bathing and eat nothing but delivery pizza while I refuse all visitors and phone calls, then don't. I've worked too hard to create this business, and I intend to keep it going."

"I'm glad, but—"

"I know what you're saying, Rosie, and don't think I won't grieve a little. He's an amazing guy. But I won't let him or anyone destroy the life I've made for myself."

"Good." Rosie gave a curt nod and picked up her coffee. "But I can't believe how stubborn he's become about his perfect life over there in California. How perfect can it be when he's by himself all the time?"

Phil refused to think of Damon with someone else. Too depressing. "I can't answer that question. I only know that if that's what he wants, that's what he should have."

Rosie contemplated her over the rim of her mug. "This might seem like it comes out of left field, but I hope I get to meet your dad someday."

"I'm sure you will. He and my stepmom are due for another trip here this fall."

"Good. Once you have dates confirmed, let me know. When he's in town, we always seem to have something going on, and we can't manage to get together. But he must be one hell of a guy."

"He is."

"I mentioned him because I suspect he's at least partly responsible for your resilience."

"Oh, definitely. He's one of the most positive people I know. He taught me early that if I'm knocked down, I have to get right back up again. He believes I can do anything."

"That's the kind of confidence I've tried to give my boys, but some of them are so damaged. Damon's parents, if you can even call them that, were—" She hesitated. "On second thought, maybe it's best if I let him tell you, if he wants to. He doesn't talk about it often. Lexi knows, and obviously so do his blood brothers."

"His what?"

"Blood brothers."

"I've never heard them mentioned before."

"Something else that's better for him to tell you than me. But I'm talking about Cade and Finn. I don't think you've met Finn."

"He's the one with the microbrewery in Seattle, right?"

"Right. The one who came up with our Kickstarter idea, which we're all hoping will work."

"And it's going to, Rosie."

She responded with a warm smile. "I'd expect you to say that, and I'm sure it will, but even if it doesn't, having those three boys around more often brings me such joy. I shouldn't have favorites, but they were the first three. If I get to see them a few times a year, I can live with giving up the ranch."

"You won't have to." Phil had championed the cause all along, but getting to know Damon made her even more determined that Rosie and Herb wouldn't lose the ranch. She couldn't bear to think of how Damon would react to that.

"With all the good people behind us, we should succeed, but I learned a big lesson from this. I'm telling everyone these days to make sure they understand their investments. Herb and I turned everything over to a friend and didn't think about it anymore."

Phil sucked in a breath. She'd never heard the details of why Rosie and Herb were nearly penniless. "Your broker was crooked?"

"Heavens, no. But he allowed himself to be dazzled by a Ponzi scheme. The enthusiasm he had for that investment was catching, and we figured he knew what he was doing. He didn't. He's devastated, both for our sake and his. He lost his shirt, too. So be careful."

"I am. I manage my own investments."

Rosie laughed. "I'm not surprised. Guess who else does?"

"Damon?"

"Yep. He doesn't have a lot invested, but he handles it himself. He offered to give us every penny, of course, but I told him if he did, I'd never speak to him again." Her gaze grew soft. "He's a good boy."

The tenderness in that phrase warmed Phil's heart. "Yes, he is. So please don't be angry with him on my account. I love that you're feeling protective of me. I never knew what it was like to have a mom, and being around you is the closest thing I've ever had to that, but—"

"That means a lot to me." Rosie's eyes grew moist. "I think of Lexi like a daughter, but she has a mom, and a good one, too. With you, I don't feel so much like I'm poaching, although I wish you could be closer to your stepmom."

"I'm working on it, and she's great for my dad, but she and I are so different. She likes to give fancy dress parties, and I'm more casual. She loves shopping in a big city, and I'd rather hang out in a small town. The main thing we have in common is we both love my dad, but that's about it."

"You know, that's probably enough. You don't have to be best friends, I guess."

"That's what I've finally decided. As long as my dad's happy, I'm happy for him. Anyway, please don't blame Damon for leading me astray. I'm a big girl. If I didn't want to risk getting involved with him, I'd just say no."

After exchanging a few last words with Rosie and giving her a hug, Phil headed back down to the meadow and was greeted by the sight of Damon pacing restlessly around the unfinished cabin, obviously impatient for her return. God, but he was yummy to look at. Saying no to a man like Damon wouldn't have been easy.

He started toward her, his long strides covering the distance quickly. His chest heaved, probably more from nervousness than exertion. The man was in perfect shape. The way his white T-shirt stretched across his shoulders and molded to his sculpted pecs was pure eye candy, and she gobbled it up.

About three feet away, he came to a halt and held up his hand like a traffic cop. "Hang on a sec."

"Why? What's the matter?" She stopped walking.

"Nothing." He adjusted the fit of his straw hat and pulled the brim lower over his eyes. "I need to get myself together before you come any closer. As I walked over here I found myself anticipating how good you'd feel in my arms. But we saw where that leads, so I'm not going to touch you at all, even though that's what I want to do."

"Okay. Good plan." She was having a similar difficulty. She felt like wrapping him in her arms, too, and not doing it seemed wrong.

But they'd just discovered how strong the chemistry was between them, so any contact would be potentially explosive. Maybe by tomorrow they'd be less volatile together. Or not. She had a tough time believing she'd ever look at him and not want to strip him naked.

He took a deep breath and glanced up. "I'm better now. How did it go with Rosie?"

"The one thing I can say with absolute certainty is that she loves you very much."

The tension eased from his expression. "I know," he said gently. "Everything she says or does is out of love. She really thinks I'm making a big mistake doing things my way."

"You're right. She does. She wants the best for you and—" Phil couldn't help smiling "—she's convinced I'm it."

He returned her smile. "She told me the same thing, and I agree with her. You're perfect. It's just that I—"

"You're not in the market for perfect."

"Not on a permanent basis." He paused and his gaze heated. "But I sure am right this minute. I am so in the market for you right now, Philomena."

Her body tightened, wanting him. She ignored it. "That's my cue. Hop to it, Harrison. We have a cabin to build."

"Just waitin' on you to say the word, Turner." He winked at her before starting back toward the site. "Only a little ways to go and we'll be ready for those windows."

She fell into step beside him. "I figured we'd get them in today. Then we can show it off tonight."

"Yeah, we should, come to think of it. Several of the people who've donated will be here. They'd probably like to see some physical evidence of progress."

"Rosie and Herb didn't mention that to me, but they probably didn't want us to feel pushed."

"I'll bet you're right." He glanced over at her. "So you and Rosie settled everything?"

"I think so. I said getting involved with you was totally under my control, and if I'd thought it was a bad idea, I would have told you no."

"And she accepted that?"

"She seemed to."

"Huh. Well, that's good, then. Because it's you, she probably believed it. I'm glad she did. That should help a lot."

"Why wouldn't she believe it?"

He turned to her with a mischievous grin. "Well, I don't like to brag, but since it's common knowledge around here, maybe it doesn't count as bragging. I'm surprised she didn't mention it."

"What?"

"When it comes to the ladies, I've never had a single one tell me no."

9

THE DAY BEFORE, Damon had given himself some ogling time. Today he hadn't dared. Now that he knew the joy of thrusting his eager cock into Philomena's welcoming warmth, he had to keep focused on the job at all times. To let his concentration falter would invite, if not disaster, then coupling on the concrete.

He might have been able to talk her into it, but he wasn't going to. Way too public for his tastes. He hadn't suggested taking a more private break inside his cabin, either. Getting all the windows in would give them both a feeling of accomplishment, and they'd need until quitting time at four to manage that.

At least that was what he'd originally estimated. He hadn't counted on Phil's efficiency. All four windows were in and framed when he checked the time on his phone. A little past three. Wow.

His shirt was plastered to his chest, and now that he allowed himself to notice, so was hers. She'd put on a ball cap once the sun had come up and had pulled her hair through the opening in back. A darkened ring around the base of the cap showed how much she'd been sweating.

She grinned at him. "Not bad, huh?"

"I thought we'd be here another hour, at least."

"I'm good at windows."

"So I see." He could see other things, too, like the outline of her bra under her damp blue T-shirt. The shirt bordered on transparent. Sweat had collected in a tiny pool at the base of her throat. Her face was flushed, which made her freckles stand out. "Guess we should get cleaned up for the party."

"Guess so." Her blue eyes darkened slightly, and then she glanced away. "You know what? I went into your cabin this morning to look for you and I think I might've dropped my keys in there. I should go check." She started over in that direction.

His heart began to pound. He didn't believe for one second that she'd dropped her keys without noticing. He could only think of one reason she'd want to go into his cabin. "Need some help looking for them?"

"Sure." She pulled off her ball cap and ran her fingers through her hair as she kept walking. "Two pairs of eyes are always better than one."

Lust slammed into him. Apparently, she didn't care that he was sweaty and grimy and decidedly fragrant. Maybe she even *liked* it. That was the most arousing thought he'd had since he'd met her, and he'd had plenty of arousing thoughts.

If she wasn't worried about a little mingled sweat and the fine grit of sawdust, then she'd just blown past all the women he'd ever gone to bed with. If she actually *preferred* making love to a man who came to her straight from a hard day of manual labor, she was one of a kind. Primitive urges stirred in him, emotions strange and wonderful.

He followed her, but the steel rod that used to be his cock made walking tough. He didn't mind at all, because soon he wouldn't have that problem. Five minutes ago he'd desperately wanted a long, cool shower. Now all he wanted was Philomena, hot, wet and willing.

Because her stride wasn't impaired like his, she made it through the door first. He was treated to the sight of her stripping off her T-shirt and tossing it to the floor, followed by her bra.

The gesture inspired him in more ways than one. He kicked the door shut. "Find your keys already?"

"Still looking." She sat on the desk chair, the same one they'd ridden to glory early that morning, and pulled off her boots. Then she lifted her gaze. Her eyes darkened to navy as she surveyed him from head to foot. "I haven't searched your bed." Her voice was a soft purr. "They might be there."

"I wouldn't doubt it." The keys to everything he ever wanted might be found there in the next few minutes. He might unlock the secrets of the universe when he was deep inside her sweet body. "I'll check." Walking over to his bunk, he yanked the mattress onto the floor. He couldn't imagine why he hadn't thought of that in the first place.

"You're very thorough."

He turned to discover that she'd peeled off her jeans and panties. He'd never seen her naked in daylight. It might be his favorite view so far. She had T-shirt tan lines that matched his, but where the sun hadn't reached, cinnamon freckles dusted her creamy skin.

He tucked that information away for tonight, because she wasn't going to give him time to kiss all those freckles now. Hunger blazed in her eyes as she came toward him.

"I couldn't wait until later," she murmured, "not when every time I looked at your hot, sweaty body, all I could think about was this." Grabbing fistfuls of his shirt, she wrenched it free of his jeans and slid her hands underneath. "Incidentally, my box of condoms is in the desk drawer."

He groaned and wrapped his arms around her, mesmerized by the fire in her eyes and the urgency in her touch as she massaged his chest. His cock surged against his fly in protest at being confined, but he didn't want to stop her from fulfilling whatever fantasy had been in her head today.

"You are so gorgeous, so...*lickable*." She shoved the material up and began to demonstrate what she meant. She used her tongue, but also her teeth, nibbling and tasting as if she couldn't get enough of him.

And he loved it. Even though he trembled with the effort to hold back, even though he longed to haul her down to the floor and take her, he stood still and let her lick his salty skin. He'd never had a woman assault him after he'd put in a long day. The sunlight filtering through the window, the sound of birds outside and the warm breeze made the moment seem more forbidden and erotic than he would have dreamed.

But at last he reached the limits of his control. "Phil...I can't wait anymore."

She looked up through her lashes, and her voice was pure seduction. "Then take me."

Cupping her bottom, he lifted her up and she wrapped her legs around his hips. He carried her to the mattress and crouched, laying her down. He yanked open the desk drawer where she'd hidden the condoms, and grabbed the box.

"See, you did need them."

"Yeah." He could barely breathe from wanting her. Setting the box down, he stood and pulled his shirt over his head. Instead of worrying about his boots and jeans, he settled for efficiency. Unfastening the snap and his fly was enough.

As he rolled on a condom, he kept his gaze on her. He'd never forget how she looked right now—her cheeks pink, her lips parted, her breasts quivering with every rapid breath and her hips moving restlessly against the rumpled bedspread. He especially wouldn't forget this midafternoon view of the curls at the juncture of her thighs and the dampness that telegraphed her desire.

He would love to give her the kind of tongue bath she'd given him, but they were running out of time. The chance that someone would wander down here to check on them was too great. He moved between her soft thighs and leaned forward, his mouth hovering over hers. "I know where your keys are."

"Where?" She caressed his back and shoulders.

"In your truck, under the seat, where you usually put them."

Her soft chuckle was sexy as hell. "Fancy that."

"Yeah, fancy that." And as he kissed her, he rocked his hips forward and shoved deep. Heaven. Good thing he'd thought to cover her mouth with his, though, because she arched against him and came with a muffled cry. His blood sang in triumph.

Lifting his head, he gazed down at her. "That was quick."

She gulped for air. "I've been…thinking about it…all day."

"Then I'll bet you can join me in another one." He began to move.

"Could be." Clutching his hips, she held his gaze as she matched his rhythm, rising to meet each thrust.

He watched her eyes darken, which was so much easier in natural light. He'd never cared what time he had sex with a woman. With Philomena, he would always choose days over nights. As he stroked faster, her eyes told him that her orgasm was drawing close.

So was his. But he could hold off long enough to let her go first. "I want to watch you come."

"I'll bet I turn red."

He smiled. "I'll bet you do." He pumped a little faster.

Her breathing changed and she tightened her grip on his hips. She was almost there. "Don't watch."

"Let me."

"Okay." She began to pant. "If you have to." She closed her eyes.

"No, don't close your eyes."

She lifted her lashes.

His breath caught. Her gaze was intense, burning with the same fire that drove him to plunge into her again and again. But within that flame was a hint of something else, a flash of vulnerability. Then she let go, surrendering to the contractions that rolled over his cock. Her face might have turned red. He couldn't say. All his attention was focused on the depth of emotion in her dark blue eyes.

As he absorbed the power of that emotion, his control slipped. Before he could regain it, his climax roared through him with a force that left him quivering and gasping for air. But he didn't look away, didn't want to. Something stirred in his chest, an unfamiliar feeling he couldn't identify.

Cradling his face in both hands, she searched his expression, a bemused smile on her kiss-reddened lips. "Are you okay?"

"Um, sure." But something had changed a moment ago, and he needed some alone time to think about what it was.

"You seem…" She paused to clear her throat. "You seem a little overwhelmed."

He tried to lighten the mood. "Who wouldn't be? A beautiful woman thinks I'm lickable when I'm covered with sweat and construction dust."

"There wasn't any dust on your chest. I probably wouldn't have licked your bare arm."

"Yeah, but I was sweaty and you didn't seem to care. That was a little mind-blowing."

She gave a little shrug. "I can't explain it. I don't get turned on by sweaty men in general, but I sure do with you, for some reason."

"My good luck, I guess." He leaned down and brushed his mouth over hers. "We'd better bring this little incident to a close, though."

"Right."

He lifted his head and looked into her eyes again. His reaction wasn't quite as intense this time, which was comforting. "At least we won't be so desperate for each other by the time the party's over."

"Funny, but I didn't even think about that. I just… needed you."

His chest tightened at the honesty of that statement.

She'd needed him and wasn't afraid to say so. He was aware that needing and wanting weren't exactly the same thing. "Good thing we finished up early."

"I was motivated. And now I'm motivated to get myself home so I can show up all cute and perky for the barbecue."

"Then I'd better let you up." After one last lingering kiss, he left their makeshift bed and turned away to dispose of the condom.

"Putting the mattress on the floor was brilliant."

"Thanks." He zipped up and turned back as she walked over to her pile of clothes. A shaft of sunlight touched her hair, highlighting the coppery glints in the deep red color. He'd taken a step toward her, hand outstretched, before he caught himself. *Look but don't touch, Harrison.*

His fascination with her was worrying, but he blamed it on the unusual circumstances. Once he left here next week and returned to his normal routine, he'd be fine. But he kept thinking of the way she'd looked at him right before her orgasm gripped her. Her gaze had been both passionate and open.

She'd claimed that they'd suffer equally when he went back to California, but he wasn't so sure. She might not be as good at building walls as he was.

"Let me help you straighten this place up."

He snapped out of his daze to discover she was dressed and headed for the mattress. "Don't bother." He blocked her path. "You have to drive home and back but all I have to do is shower and change. I'll take care of it."

"All right." She peered at him. "Are you sure you're okay?"

"I'm fine, but I'm worried about you."

"Me? I'm terrific. Couldn't be better."

"I think…" He hesitated. This could be an explosive situation, one he didn't have a lot of practice in dealing with. "I think being with me could be bad for you. In the long run."

She crossed her arms. "And what brought you to that conclusion?"

He wasn't going to tell her what he'd seen in her eyes when they were making love. That seemed too tender and personal. So he latched on to something else. "A little while ago you said you *needed* me. That doesn't sound like the statement of somebody who will go merrily on her way after I leave."

"Oh, for heaven's sake. Now we're debating word choices. After working with you all day and observing your bodacious physique, I *needed* a release. I said I needed *you*, because it sounds really crass to say that I needed sex with the nearest available man, which happened to be you."

He didn't believe a word of it, but he couldn't argue the point without bringing up what he'd seen in her eyes right before she gave herself to an orgasm that he'd helped create. A gentleman didn't do that to a lady. "I'm just checking, because I don't want you to be… unhappy."

"We've already discussed that. Of course I'll be unhappy for a little while. Most people would be. But as I told Rosie, I'm not about to let you or any guy sabotage the life I've worked so hard to build."

He took note of the belligerent jut of her chin and the defiant gleam in her eyes. There was nothing open and vulnerable about her now. Maybe she could build psychological walls as well as she constructed real ones. "That's great. Glad to hear it."

"Were you leading up to something, like maybe you shouldn't spend the night at my house?"

"Well, I—"

"Because frankly, you're beginning to worry *me*. I catch you staring off into space and acting as if something's really bothering you. Are you afraid you're getting in too deep with me? If so, we can dial it back. I don't want to hurt you, either."

That pricked his manly pride. "Like I've said, I won't enjoy leaving you, and I'll miss you, but I can handle it."

"Then I guess neither of us has to worry about the other one."

"Guess not."

"So the invitation is still open, if you care to take advantage of it." Her blue gaze challenged him. "You'll be the first man to christen my sleigh bed, if that interests you at all."

He smiled. "I guess you do know guys pretty well. Not many of us could resist being the first guy in a woman's cherished sleigh bed."

"Just so you don't get the wrong impression, you're not the first one to be invited. But the others declined. Wait, that sounds as if I've issued invitations right and left. In the past five years, I've invited two different guys to share that bed. In each case, they declined."

"Why the hell would they do that?"

"I can't tell you for sure, but I think they didn't want to be confronted with my expertise as a carpenter and general handywoman. If we stayed in their apartment, they could maintain their illusion of superiority in all areas."

"What a load of bull. I can't wait to see what you've done with your place."

Her voice softened. "And I can't wait to show it to you. It's not often I can entertain someone who understands what went into the renovation. My dad's visited, and he's appreciative, but he's my dad. He'd rave if I put new hinges on the front door."

He'd always suspected that more was riding on his overnights at her house than simply sex. Phil wanted to show off her work, and boy, did he understand that. It was the driving reason he flipped houses. If no one ever saw the result of your labors, what was the point?

Walking over to her, he drew her into his arms. "Enough of the psychoanalyzing. I want to come home with you tonight. I want to see all the great things you've done with your house. And then I want to kiss every freckle on your sweet body."

She blushed. "And now you have a general idea of how many that is."

"The more to tease you with, my dear." He gave her a goodbye kiss and she left the cabin. He watched her go and hoped he was doing the right thing, both for her and for him. If she was falling for him, he'd never forgive himself. If he was falling for her...that would be a first. He'd never allowed it to happen before, but he'd never met anyone like Philomena, either.

He felt restless, in need of an activity that would take his mind off her, and he knew exactly what he craved. After pulling on his T-shirt and retrieving his hat, he walked down to the barn, where he met his foster father.

"Finished for the day?" Herb asked.

"We are. How's the automatic watering system working?"

"Better, but I'm still not happy with it."

"I'll take a look before I head back to California."

"That would be great. Don't worry about it now, though. Rosie made me promise I wouldn't be in the middle of fixing it when the party starts, and I'm sure that goes for you, too."

"I wasn't thinking of doing it now, but I sure would like to borrow your horse for a little while if that's okay."

"You know it is, son. Just don't be gone too long or Rosie will start fretting. You know how she gets before a party."

Damon laughed. "I know. I just need to blow off some steam."

"That sounds great. Wish I could go with you, but Rosie wants me up at the house to help her with the tables."

"Oh. Well, I could help with that, too."

"No, no. Go for your ride. You don't get much chance to do that anymore, I'll bet."

"No, I sure don't."

"Then go and have fun."

"That's the idea." Damon grabbed a lead rope from the barn and walked out to the pasture with a sense of anticipation. Moments later he had Navarre, a dark chestnut, tethered to the hitching post.

Saddling and bridling the horse reminded him of how much he missed doing this task. He'd considered checking out stables in the LA area but instinctively he'd known they wouldn't provide the experience he was looking for. Mounting up and trotting away from the barn made him smile with pleasure.

He headed across ranch property toward a gate that

opened out on Forest Service land and a primitive dirt road leading into the trees. Once they were through the gate and on the road, Navarre trotted faster of his own accord. Damon chuckled. "Guess you need to blow off some steam, too, huh? Okay, buddy, let's go!" He nudged the horse's flanks and Navarre leaped forward.

Grabbing his hat, Damon held it against his chest as they pounded down the dirt road at a full gallop. Oh, yeah. He'd needed this. Surfing was fun, but it didn't thrill him like a hard ride on a good horse. At heart, he would always be a cowboy.

10

PHIL HAD BEEN to several parties at Thunder Mountain Ranch and they'd always been joyous affairs. The Padgetts knew how to entertain and make people feel welcome and special. But this particular party felt bittersweet. The guests all knew that if Thunder Mountain Academy didn't raise enough money by the Kickstarter deadline of September first, this would be the last party at the ranch.

Because of that, everyone was eager to see what she and Damon had done so far. The fourth cabin provided visible evidence that steps were being taken to save the ranch. Rosie asked if Phil and Damon would take any interested guests on a tour while she and Herb finished setting out the food. Lexi had arrived early, and she and Cade had already checked on the cabin's progress, so they offered to help Herb and Rosie.

Phil was happy to play tour guide. She was proud of the work they'd done. But there was a strange vibe going on between her and Damon. She had a hunch what it was all about—he was becoming emotionally involved with her and didn't know how to handle it.

She'd have to let him worry about that, though. She had enough problems with her own emotions. They were all over the place. She'd never been as forward with a man as she had been with Damon right from the beginning.

He was probably used to women coming on strong, but no guy had ever inspired her to behave this way. She'd driven out to his cabin, for pity's sake, wearing nothing but a caftan and flip-flops. She'd started the encounter in the bathhouse, and this afternoon she'd deliberately seduced him.

She blamed her sense of urgency on the ticking clock, which certainly had something to do with it. But the truth was, she'd fallen in lust with him from the get-go and it was threatening to turn into something deeper. She wondered if the same thing was happening to him.

He wouldn't want to acknowledge that in himself, so he'd shifted all his uneasiness onto her. If she said the word, he'd nobly end their affair for her own good. Glancing at Damon as they led a group of party guests out to the cabin, she was glad she'd managed to talk him out of it. She'd been crazy for him this afternoon in his sweat-soaked T-shirt and worn jeans, but this presentation had great appeal, too. He'd borrowed a black felt hat from somebody, and his black Western shirt with silver piping emphasized the breadth of his shoulders. His black dress jeans emphasized...*oh, yeah*.

She'd waited so long for the right guy to join her in that sleigh bed. Now that she'd met someone who wasn't intimidated by her, she'd enjoy the experience until it ended. No expectations and no regrets.

Although she loved being alone with him, watching him interact with the folks at the party was fun, too. At the moment he was talking earnestly with Ty Slater, a former Thunder Mountain foster kid. Phil knew from Rosie that he was now a successful attorney in Cheyenne, but the guy looked like a cowboy to her. He wore his brown Stetson with authority, and he was obviously used to walking around in boots, jeans and a yoked Western shirt.

Ty was handling the legal paperwork for Thunder Mountain Academy's Kickstarter program. Phil wasn't surprised that Damon was quizzing him. Damon wouldn't want to leave any legal detail hanging.

Molly, Cade's long-lost cousin, came up beside Phil. "I know we've met a few times," she said, "but I don't think Ben's ever been with me."

Phil smiled at the tall cowboy. "We haven't met, but I've heard great things about your saddles."

"And I've heard great things about your home repair skills." He returned her smile. "So far I've been stubbornly handling those chores myself, but Rosie keeps telling me you'd do a better job and a lot faster, too."

"Rosie likes to promote small businesses, and I love her for it. If I ever learn to ride well enough to buy a horse, I know who I'll ask to build my saddle."

"Ben's an artist." Molly's eyes, the exact same green as Cade's, glowed with love. "Whoever's lucky enough to take his class on saddle-making at the academy is going to learn from the best."

"That's exciting." Phil admired Molly's confidence that the academy would become a reality. "So how's the curriculum shaping up?"

"It'll be amazing." Molly had left a job teaching history at a community college in Arizona to marry Ben, and she'd landed a part-time position at Sheridan Community College. She was devoting all her extra hours to developing Thunder Mountain Academy's schedule of classes in order to get state accreditation.

"I wish I could be sixteen again," Phil said. "The program sounds like fun. Rosie told me five kids from back East have already registered for the spring session."

"They have. And more will soon, I'm sure. I know the contributions aren't quite where Rosie and Herb would like to see them at this stage, but— Oh, my goodness. I didn't realize you'd have windows in already!" Molly stopped to stare at the half-finished cabin. "I just got chills. It's really happening."

The awe in Molly's voice was touching. Phil glanced around and noticed that guests were exploring the site with smiles on their faces. Several had walked inside the cabin and were waving to others through the new windows. The buzz of happy conversation was punctuated with laughter. So many people loved Rosie and Herb and wanted Thunder Mountain Academy to succeed.

"It looks great, Phil." Ben gazed at the cabin. "It's a lot to have accomplished in two days. You and Damon must work well together."

"We do." She hoped her expression didn't give too much away.

"He's a good guy," Molly said. "Cade says he wouldn't be the person he is today without Damon and Finn. He says that Damon—"

"Hang on." Damon came over with Ty. First he made the introductions, and then he gestured toward Molly. "Okay, you can continue bragging on me now. Ty thinks of me as the guy who pulled all kinds of pranks and refuses to believe I've become an upstanding citizen. I'd appreciate it if you'd set him straight."

Ty shrugged. "That's just how I remember it. Cade had the stash of rubber snakes, and you were forever short-sheeting the beds. I think Finn was the one who glued the toilet seats shut, but that could've been you, too. And somebody put salt in the sugar bowl, and there was the time you duct-taped our cabin door shut, and—"

"Molly, tell him I've reformed."

She laughed. "I wish I could say that, but Lexi mentioned that Cade still has some of those rubber snakes, so I have to assume that you—"

"Nope, nope." He held up both hands. "I can't speak for Cade and Finn, but I'm a changed man." He glanced over at Phil. "You've spent two days working with me. Tell them I'm a serious, hardworking dude."

"No pranks so far, but the week's not over. Sounds as if I'd better stay alert."

Ty chuckled. "I would if I were you. I lived with this guy for…how long was it?"

"Not long enough, apparently. You totally misjudged my sterling character."

"Three years. I came when I was fifteen and left for college when I was eighteen. And you were pulling stuff the entire time, my friend."

Damon rolled his eyes. "Selective memory."

"Photographic memory."

"Damn. I forgot about that. Listen, could we change the subject?"

"Consider it done. I have something I wanted to discuss with Ben, anyway. Rosie said you had a concern about liability if you teach the saddle-making classes in your shop."

Ben nodded. "Yeah, I do."

Damon clapped Ty on the shoulder. "Then if you'll

excuse me while you do your lawyer thing, I need to have a little chat with Phil about tomorrow's work schedule."

"Sure." Ty glanced at him. "I'll catch up with you later."

"You bet." Damon took Phil's elbow. "Let's move out of traffic." He guided her several feet away from the crowd.

"What about the work schedule? Is there a problem? All the materials are there. I thought we'd finish the walls, frame the door and start on the—"

"We will." He released her elbow. "All that. I just needed a moment to tell you…you look so beautiful."

Her breath stalled. "Thank you. It's just my normal nice clothes. Nothing special."

"You make them special." He smiled. "I like the bling on the back pockets of your jeans, not that I needed anything sparkly to draw my attention to that spot."

Her cheeks warmed. She was guilty of wearing those jeans because she wanted him to be teased, just a little bit, by the flash of sequins.

"Philomena, you have one fine—"

"Shh." She glanced around, but nobody seemed to be listening. She'd achieved her goal of making him notice, and now they should dial it back.

"Well, you do. So soft, and yet firm and extremely kissable. I—"

"Damon." Her little ploy had succeeded far better than she'd anticipated.

But he wasn't finished. "It's not only the jeans that caught my attention. It's also your green silk shirt. It is silk, right? Like your caftan? Because it reminds me of the way the caftan draped your—"

"Yes, it's silk." She looked everywhere but at him.

"Listen, I admit that I wore the silk shirt because of the caftan, but that's enough of this talk. We're in public."

"Nobody knows what I'm saying."

"I do." She risked glancing up. And she forgot that anyone else existed.

His warm gray eyes drew her in, reminding her of the pleasure they'd shared only hours ago, and the pleasure they would find in her bed tonight. Whatever tension she'd felt coming from him a little while ago seemed to have vanished. Now he was all in, committed to turning her on, committed to spending the night making glorious love to her.

She cleared her throat. "If you were trying to get me hot, you succeeded."

"I was." He smiled. "You looked so calm and collected from the front. I didn't notice the bling until I saw you over there talking to Molly and Ben. And then I hoped you'd worn it for me."

"Actually, I did."

"So you were trying to get *me* hot."

She laughed. "Guess so."

"Worked like a charm. I—" A distant dinner bell sounded. "Looks like we'd better head back. Just so you know, I planned that we'd sit together."

"I'd like that." She looked forward to the feast-like atmosphere. Traditionally, Rosie and Herb set up rows of folding tables and chairs in a side yard adjacent to the house. Food was always plentiful, which made the table legs sink into the soft earth from the weight of the platters lined up down the middle of each row.

As she and Damon walked past the house, several people stopped them to comment on a job well-done.

A few added specific observations about the troweling on the cement or the professional window install.

"Phil gets the credit for that," Damon said whenever someone praised something she'd been specifically instrumental in doing.

After the fourth time he'd said it, she spoke up. "It's a shared project. You can just say thank you."

"I know I could, but what if some of these people think like I used to? What if they assume I did all the hard stuff and you only helped?"

"What if they do? So what?"

"They need to adjust their thinking, that's what." He sounded truly indignant.

And that was the moment she fell in love with Damon Harrison. She'd been edging in that direction, but that comment pushed her right over the cliff. She couldn't call it lust anymore.

Well, it qualified as lust, too, but the basic emotion, the one driving the bus, was love. She'd keep it to herself, though. Talk about a buzzkill. If she ever spoke that word aloud, he'd vacate her sleigh bed faster than a speeding bullet.

"You see what I'm saying, right?" He glanced at her as if expecting a response. "People can't go on assuming things that are wrong. That's not good."

Her throat was tight from the feelings he'd churned up, but she managed to agree with him.

"Are you okay?" He was looking at her in obvious concern. "You're not coming down with something, are you?"

"No, I feel fine."

"I wondered, because your voice sounded a little raspy just now, and I'd hate for you to get sick."

"I'm not getting sick."

"It wouldn't be a surprise if you were. Hard work, not much sleep. Promise you'll tell me if you start feeling bad."

"I'm fine." And she wouldn't promise him a damned thing. She was likely to start feeling bad after his plane took off from the Sheridan County Airport, and she sure as hell wouldn't tell him about that.

"Good." He lowered his voice. "Just so you know, I planned on some sleeping tonight along with…the other."

"Did you, now?" She managed to keep from laughing.

"That may not work out. But we really should get some sleep, don't you think?"

"Probably, especially if we're going to be climbing around on the rafters tomorrow."

"Good point. You don't want to be doing that tired." He hesitated. "I had this idea, but you might not want to do it."

"You want to paint every other log purple."

"Be serious."

"You're right. That would be dumb. You'd have to paint every log purple or it just wouldn't look right."

"Never mind. I'll tell you later."

"No, tell me now. I'm sorry. I'll stop goofing around. I think I'm getting punchy."

"Which is why we need to sleep. Except I don't know if I can if you're right there, so…*available.*"

She longed for a way to record this crazy conversation. "What's your idea? Please tell me."

"Okay, I was thinking that after we finished the

cabin and the lock is on the door, we should carry a mattress in there and...celebrate."

Her chest tightened. "I love that idea."

"I'm glad. So do I. It's our project, and we should be the ones to commemorate a job well-done. Just the two of us."

"Absolutely." She was convinced that he'd never allowed himself to fall in love before, and he was in denial that it was happening now. Someone, Cade or Lexi or Rosie, might suggest that was his problem. She hoped they wouldn't. If anyone put a label on what he was feeling, he'd take off.

Sure, he'd leave for California in a few days, anyway, but no point in ruining what was going on until then. She was content in her knowledge that they were both in love, even if he studiously ignored the possibility. Maybe they'd only have tonight to experience that special feeling before someone or something spoiled it. If so, she'd take it as a gift and be grateful. Some people never had that much.

11

DAMON SOAKED UP the nostalgia of a Fourth of July barbecue at Thunder Mountain Ranch. His ride this afternoon, followed by the kind of celebration he'd loved as a teenager, made him wish he didn't live quite so far away. He couldn't duplicate any of this in California.

The tables were lit with old-fashioned kerosene lamps just as he remembered, and the Independence Day–themed tablecloths were in use, even though they were a bit the worse for wear. The food was pure Americana—ears of corn, ribs, sliced tomatoes, fried chicken, baked beans, potato salad and coleslaw. Watermelon was served for dessert, along with apple and cherry pie à la mode.

Cade and Lexi claimed a spot opposite Damon and Phil. Ty and Brant joined them, although Damon made sure Phil was on his left, away from those guys. He hadn't thoroughly examined that impulse, mostly because he'd rather not. He suspected that once he did, he wouldn't be pleased with himself.

But for now, the beer was flowing, and he could ignore his instant dislike of any man who gave Phil a second look. She was by his side, her hip against his hip, her arm brushing his arm, and that seemed right to him. If she was happy with the short-term arrangement between them, so was he.

Herb made a little speech thanking everyone for their support of Thunder Mountain Academy. Then Rosie passed out T-shirts to everyone decorated with the academy's logo, an inverted horseshoe with TMA arranged at the top to create snow-capped mountain peaks. The T-shirts were a huge hit, and some people put them on over whatever they were wearing. Camera phones appeared, and several group pictures were taken.

Damon remembered first seeing that logo, designed by Molly's husband, Ben, the day Rosie had been discharged from the hospital. So much had happened since then. The Kickstarter project was up and running, and Cade was almost engaged to Lexi. Although she hadn't asked him, Damon saw how they acted with each other. It was only a matter of time.

Rosie's health had started improving from the moment the Thunder Mountain Brotherhood had rallied to help her save the ranch. Damon had reinforced his connection with Cade and Finn, something he'd meant to do ever since they'd all left Thunder Mountain. And because of a glitch in his renovation schedule, he'd met Philomena Turner.

She pulled her T-shirt on over that sexy green blouse, which made her look adorably nerdy. As she ran her fingers through her hair, she glanced at him. "Aren't you going to put yours on?"

"I don't think it'll fit over my shirt. I might rip it."

"So take your other shirt off first."

"Here?"

Cade stood and started unbuttoning his shirt. "Good idea. I don't want to rip the shirt, either, and besides, Lexi never tires of seeing my manly chest."

Lexi groaned. "Get out the shovels. Here comes a load of—"

"Great idea." Ty took off his hat and unsnapped his cuffs. "You know what? We should do a beefcake calendar as one of the incentives for our Kickstarter backers. Brant, you up for that?"

"You bet." Brant Ellison, who worked as a wrangler on a ranch near Cody, also stood and started taking off his shirt. "We could call it *The Men of Thunder Mountain*."

"Ooo, I like it!" Molly called over to them. "Ben's in."

"Aw, Molly, I'm—"

"Come on, Ben," Lexi said. "It's for a good cause."

"But I never lived on the ranch."

"No," Molly said, "but you're a key person for the academy, and you're gorgeous. You belong on this calendar."

Lexi nodded. "That's right. Damon, what are you stalling for? Off with your shirt. Don't let Cade upstage you."

"Which I totally could with my rippling abs." Cade launched into a series of elaborate bodybuilding poses.

That brought laughter and wolf whistles from the crowd, and a couple of women started a rhythmic clap. Soon every woman in the crowd joined in, including Molly and Phil. With a self-conscious smile, Ben stood and handed Molly his hat.

Damon glanced at Phil, who stopped clapping long

enough to give him a thumbs-up. He gave her his hat and started in on his buttons.

"Look at that, Rosie!" Molly seemed beside herself with excitement. "We have January through May right here."

Rosie surveyed the five of them. "We certainly do! Ty, since this is your brilliant idea, I'd like you to be in charge of rounding up seven more brothers to finish the calendar."

"Be glad to." Ty put on his T-shirt. "As long as you have some contact info."

"I'll get it now. If we want to use it as a thank-you for contributors, we have to move fast. Next year's calendars are already showing up in stores." Rosie hurried into the house.

"Ty, we only need six more guys." Cade picked up his logo T-shirt and pulled it over his head. "Finn doesn't know it yet, but he's in."

"He sure is." Damon put on his T-shirt and retrieved his hat from Phil. "If we have to, he has to."

"He'll do it," Lexi said. "Chelsea will insist. Her marketing heart will fall in love with this idea. I can't wait to hear her response." She pulled out her phone. "Cade, take off your shirt again."

He preened as he surveyed the group. "See? What did I tell you? She loves my body."

"This is strictly business, cowboy." Lexi stood and turned her phone on. "Damon, take yours off, too. All of you, shirts off and hats on. Line up so I can text Chelsea a picture. She'll go nuts over this."

Damon thought so, too. Last month he, Cade, Finn and Lexi had scheduled a Skype call to Seattle so they could talk with Chelsea, the woman who'd guided

Finn through the Kickstarter campaign he'd run for his microbrewery. Chelsea understood marketing. She was also obviously in love with Finn, who'd sworn off women following his divorce earlier in the year.

The guys lined up for Lexi, and she snapped a couple of pictures. "Perfect. The lighting's not great, but she'll get the idea."

Molly came over as Damon was putting on his shirt for the second time. "Could I talk to you privately for a minute?"

"Sure." He glanced at Phil. "Excuse me for a sec."

"No worries." She stood and began gathering plates. "I'm going to help with the cleanup."

"I should—"

"It's okay." Phil smiled at him. "We have a lot of helpers."

"I guess." It went against his nature to leave that for other people, but Molly definitely had something on her mind. He could see it in her eyes. He gestured toward a spot away from the rows of tables. "That good enough?"

"That's fine. It has to do with Cade," she murmured as they walked away from the hubbub. "And this calendar idea."

"He seems to be looking forward to it." Damon wasn't, but he'd go along.

Molly laughed. "I could tell. I didn't realize he's such a ham." She paused and turned to him. "I know the perfect photographer for it, and I'm sure she'd donate her services."

"That would be great!"

"It would be except for one thing. Her name is Dominique Chance. She's Nick Chance's wife."

"Oh." Looking into Molly's eyes was always such a

shock, because they were so like Cade's. Those green eyes must be a dominant trait in the Gallagher family. "So Cade should be the one to ask."

"Yes, and the sooner, the better. Waiting until he sees them in two weeks will waste valuable time. And he hasn't even said he'd tell them about the academy when he goes over there with Lexi."

"So you want me to talk to him."

"If you would."

He sighed. "There's a reason why he's reluctant to ask them to support the academy. It might not make sense to you, but it does to me."

"I guess it's because he feels like a shirttail relative, and he doesn't want to approach them with his hand out."

"Exactly."

"They wouldn't look at it like that. They're wonderful people who'd understand that he's trying to help the family who gave him a home for so many years."

"I'll mention that to him. Are you sure you don't want to be part of the conversation?"

Molly shook her head. "He'll listen to you. I'd only be in the way. It's always been important for him to contact them about the academy, but the calendar makes it even more time-sensitive. Dominique's a pro and a fast worker. She could make the calendar happen."

Damon took off his hat and ran his fingers through his hair.

"Nice hat, by the way."

"Thanks. Herb drove into town yesterday and bought it for me. He said I couldn't wear that old straw thing to a party. I tried to pay him, but he wouldn't take it.

I'll probably get him and Rosie a gift card to a restaurant or something."

"Or you could accept the hat as a gesture of his love."

"He's already given me so much. I—"

"He wanted to buy you that hat, Damon. I'm sure he was tickled to do it. Let him."

"You're right." He smiled. "He had the cutest expression on his face when he pulled it out of the shopping bag."

"He's such a peach. Both of them are. Maybe if you approach it from that angle, that Cade needs to do this for them, he'll overcome his misgivings."

"Maybe." He put the hat on and tugged on the brim. Then he looked at her. "I know he'd want to, but when you come from rock bottom like Cade and I have, it colors everything. Asking for favors feels too much like begging, and that's the one thing neither of us ever wants to do."

"I understand."

He knew she didn't, not really. No one could understand who hadn't felt that soul-deep panic of not knowing where your next meal was coming from or where you'd end up sleeping. But she had a sympathetic nature, and that counted for a lot.

He met her gaze. "I'll talk to him. I can't promise it'll make a difference, but I'll see what I can do. Dominique sounds like a perfect choice to be the photographer."

"I guarantee she is. And she's made contacts around the state, so let's say Ty or Brant couldn't get up here for a photo shoot. Dominique would find a photographer closer to them. She'd coordinate the whole thing."

"I'll tell Cade that, too." He hoped to hell it would make a difference. But he'd been standing outside

Rosie's hospital room last month when Molly had come to visit and had bumped right into Cade, the cousin she'd given up hope of finding. That meeting had shaken the foundations of Cade's world, and he obviously hadn't adjusted to the new horizon yet.

"That's all I ask." Molly looked over at the tables, which were now empty. "Looks like we got out of cleanup duty."

"No problem." She might assume he'd be glad about that, but she didn't know him very well. Anyone who did knew that creating order out of chaos was his favorite activity. Or it had been. Making love to Philomena might be in first place now.

"Let's go see if Lexi's heard from Chelsea." Molly headed back toward the group of people standing around talking as they made preparations to leave.

Damon heard discussion about attending the fireworks show that would begin in another hour outside town. A woman Damon didn't know turned to Phil and asked her if she planned to go again this year.

"It's great," Phil said, "but Damon and I will start working tomorrow at dawn. We both want to finish that cabin before he leaves. So I'm going to make it an early night."

He smiled. Fireworks had nothing on spending the night in Philomena's sleigh bed. The party had been fun, but he was ready for it to be over.

Molly had sought out Lexi, and the two of them came back over to him.

"Chelsea loves the calendar idea," Lexi said. "I thought she would. She thinks we should get on it ASAP."

"And I told her I had the perfect photographer," Molly added, "but she happens to be a Chance."

Lexi glanced over at Cade several feet away. He was busy joking with Ty and Brant. "He's not going to want to ask her."

"I know," Damon said. "But he's holding up the works." As much as he didn't want to discuss it with Cade tonight and delay slipping away with Phil, he couldn't see any other option. He didn't know much about photography, but the timeline seemed extremely short. Molly had come up with a great solution, but if they planned to ask Dominique Chance to do it, they should ask immediately. "I'll get him off in a corner right now and explain how the cow eats the cabbage."

Lexi looked worried. "There's a lot at stake for him."

"There's a lot at stake for a whole bunch of people. I'm counting on him to realize that. Phil, I'll talk to you later, okay?"

"Sure thing." She gave him a quick smile. Rosie and Herb knew he planned to leave with her tonight. Lexi and Cade had probably figured it out. But the entire gathering didn't have to know.

Damon approached the three guys casually, as if he didn't have anything special on his mind. "So we're doing this calendar thing, huh?"

"We are." Cade grinned at him. "And I'll bet you don't wanna."

"Not especially. But if it would help Rosie and Herb, I'd strip naked in front of the church choir on Sunday morning." He was making a joke, but he was also making a point. He hoped Cade had the same mentality, although stripping naked would be easier than what Damon would ask of him.

On the spur of the moment, he decided to propose it in front of Ty and Brant. It wasn't playing fair, but he didn't want to give Cade the opportunity to say no. "Molly knows a great photographer who'll probably do it for free if we ask her."

"Oh, yeah?" Cade perked right up. "That sounds terrific. Do we know her?"

Damon hated doing this, but tough times called for tough measures. "You do, sort of. Dominique Chance. She's married to Nick, one of the Chance brothers."

"I've heard of her," Ty said. "She's getting quite a reputation for portraits of cowboys. She'd be perfect if we could even get her, which I doubt. But I don't have a clue why you think she'd do it for free."

Cade glowered at Damon. "Because her husband is my cousin."

Ty blinked. "No shit." He clapped Cade on the shoulder. "You've been holding out on me, brother. I didn't know you were so well connected."

"Turns out I am." He cleared his throat. "Will you guys excuse me and Damon? We have a few things to go over."

"Absolutely," Brant said. "I need another beer, anyway. I'm not driving anywhere tonight. But Cade, man, that would be awesome if you can get your cousin-in-law to help us out."

"Yeah." Cade jerked his head to the side to indicate Damon should follow him into the shadows. Once they were a good distance away, he whirled to face him. "What the *hell* was that all about? That was an ambush!"

"I know, and I'm sorrier than I can say. But you have to do this."

"No, I don't, and damn it, you know how I feel about this! I'm going over to meet them in two weeks, but now you're asking me to approach them, hat in hand, and—"

"Yes, I am, and I might be one of the few people here who knows what that will cost you. But it's for Rosie and Herb. You have to."

Cade crossed his arms and glared. "I thought we took an oath to protect each other."

"I am protecting you, idiot. You need to contact the Chance family anyway, to ask for their help with the campaign. Now the calendar's on the table, and Nick's wife is a crackerjack photographer. Everybody's waiting on you, hotshot. You can't stall any longer. If you do, this whole project could go down the drain and then what? Are you prepared to watch Rosie pack up and leave this place?"

"You forced my hand."

"Yes."

"That wasn't nice."

"No."

"I have half a mind to punch you."

Damon braced himself. "Go ahead, if it'll make you feel any better. But you have to make that phone call to the ranch, and it needs to be tomorrow. We're asking a huge favor of Dominique, and she deserves as much time as we can give her."

"So why didn't you tell me all this privately?"

"Would you have agreed to call, or would you have procrastinated?"

Cade blew out a breath. "Procrastinated. God, I hate that you know me so well."

"I know how hard this will be for you. In your shoes, I would have had to be forced to do it. So I decided to take away your choices and leave you with only one option, to do the right thing."

"It's the holiday weekend. I can't call about something like this on a holiday weekend."

"Cade, so help me God, if you don't call tomorrow, I'm gonna whip your butt."

His chin lifted. "You can try."

"Remember our last fight?"

"Like it was yesterday. Fall semester of our senior year, and as I recall, it was a draw."

Damon nodded. "It was."

"Herb found us in the barn, neither of us ready to give up but too tired to go on." Cade shook his head. "What a pathetic situation. Remember what it was about?"

"No, do you?"

"No." Cade laughed. "But I'm sure it was your fault."

"I so doubt that. Want to have a beer before you head over to Lexi's?"

"I could go for one. But aren't you itching to get in there and help clean up the kitchen?"

"Phil said they had plenty of helpers, and I think you and I need to have a beer." Smoothing over an argument with his blood brother was more important than kitchen duty. It was even more important than leaving right this minute with Phil. He glanced over to where she was talking with Lexi and Molly. He raised his voice. "Me and Cade are gonna grab a beer."

Phil laughed. "Fine."

"Lexi?" Cade called out. "You okay with that?"

"Sure! Enjoy. It's a holiday, after all."

"My thought exactly." Cade slung an arm over Damon's shoulder, and they walked over to the cooler to see if any beer was left. "Holidays are for hangin' out with family."

"You said it." Damon made a mental note to check with Cade tomorrow and confirm that he'd called the Last Chance Ranch.

But odds were that call would be made. Cade knew on some level that Damon wouldn't back him into a corner unless the stakes were high. They couldn't be much higher. The Brotherhood faced losing the only place any of them had been able to call home.

12

PHIL WAS FASCINATED by the interaction between Damon and Cade. She didn't have any siblings, but she'd known plenty of kids in school with brothers and sisters. The bond she'd witnessed there was a pale imitation of what she sensed between these two members of the Thunder Mountain Brotherhood.

Lexi watched them each take a beer from the cooler and grab a couple of chairs. "I'm so glad they worked it out. For a minute there, I thought they might end up slugging each other."

Molly nodded. "I've seen my brothers get that look on their faces, and nine times out of ten somebody ends up with a black eye."

"Fortunately, we were spared that," Lexi said. "And I'm happy to leave them alone to drink their beer and talk about old times. Let's go see if Rosie needs help in the kitchen."

"Sounds good." Phil wondered how mellow Damon would be by the time she took him home with her. This could be a very short night, indeed.

"So you aren't going to the fireworks?" Molly asked.

"Not me," Lexi said, "but if you and Ben plan to, you'd better get a move on."

"Okay, I will. He wants us to go together. He hasn't had anyone to share holidays with, and he's so excited about it." Molly's tender expression said it all. She was besotted by her husband.

As well she should be, Phil thought. The concept hadn't been particularly real to her before Damon, but he'd raised her expectations for the kind of passion she required in a life partner. Now she wouldn't be satisfied with anything less.

She followed Lexi into the ranch kitchen, which bustled with activity and discussion about the calendar. Ty and Brant stood at the sink washing and drying whatever hadn't fit in the dishwasher while Rosie and a couple of other women wrapped up the leftovers.

Lexi paused in the doorway, looked over at Phil and lowered her voice. "Is there anything sexier than a cowboy washing dishes?"

"Yeah. Two cowboys washing dishes."

Lexi chuckled. "I know, right? Rosie taught those boys well."

As if she'd heard her name mentioned, Rosie glanced up from the watermelon she was wrapping. "Phil, would you take this out to the overflow refrigerator? I've filled up the one in here. In fact, that's what you two girls can do to help. All this on the table needs to be stored in the second fridge."

"We're on it." Phil hefted the half a watermelon and carried it into the rec room located off the kitchen. When Phil had come out to replace the caulking around the windows, Rosie had told her how it had been added on when the population of foster boys had grown too large for everyone to be fed in the kitchen and entertained in the living room.

The pool table that dominated the space had a wooden cover that allowed it to be used as a dining table. The stained-glass fixture that hung over it was on, giving the room a cozy glow. At one time the refrigerator had been full of soda, according to Rosie. Now the shelves in the door held mostly beer bottles.

Phil stowed the watermelon and looked around. "This isn't going to be a big enough space for sixteen teenagers, especially older ones."

"I've thought about that, too." Lexi put away two covered dishes, and they walked back to the kitchen for more. "The max they housed at the ranch before was eleven, because the Brotherhood insisted only the three of them could live in their cabin."

"Really? That's cheeky."

"You have no idea. They treated it like their private clubhouse. They even carved their logo on the beam over the door."

Phil smiled. She liked hearing the stories about Damon's life here. Now she wanted to see that carving.

"And the other thing is, the boys were of varying ages, some as young as ten."

Rosie handed them each more covered dishes. "What are you two plotting? I can tell something's up."

"A rec hall." Lexi turned to Phil. "Is that what you were thinking, too?"

"Yep. You need something bigger than the rec room for those sixteen kids, especially with a mix of boys and girls. And it could double as classroom space during the day."

Rosie sighed. "I agree, but we didn't figure that into the budget."

"It might not be as expensive as you think." She picked up a covered bowl of coleslaw. "Damon and I could create a rough blueprint on my computer before he leaves. Once again, no plumbing, just electric, and if we both donate our labor, then—"

"Or I could give you more riding lessons for your part." Lexi adjusted the stack of storage dishes in her arms and added one more. "That's if you want them. I realize riding lessons don't buy groceries, but I'm offering."

"Oh, I want to! I have visions of buying a horse someday and ordering a custom saddle from Ben."

"Well, a rec hall would be wonderful if there's any way we can afford it." Rosie looked at Phil. "Damon would have to come back over here and help build it. That would be a bonus."

"Yes, it would." Phil knew she was blushing.

"Then let's see if we can make it happen. And thanks for helping store all that food. If you can make everything fit, you're a couple of wizards."

"I can do it." Phil returned her smile. "I was a whiz at Tetris."

"Hey, me, too." Lexi grinned at her. "We should play sometime."

"I'd love it." She followed Lexi back into the rec room.

"You absolutely don't have to answer this, but I'm dying of curiosity. How's it going with Damon?"

As Phil switched the containers around to maximize space, she searched for a way to explain the situation.

"Never mind. It's none of my business. Forget I asked."

"I wouldn't mind talking to somebody." She turned and took the ones Lexi handed her. "But I wouldn't want it to get back to Damon."

"If you're worried that I'd repeat whatever you told me to Cade, I won't. I know what it's like to be in love with somebody who came from a dicey background. Loving Cade hasn't been a walk in the park."

"I guess it's obvious I'm falling for him."

"To me and Rosie, but we both have inside information. I'm not sure anybody else has picked up on it."

"I hope not." Phil tucked the last bowl in the only spot left and it fit perfectly.

"You *are* good at that."

"Spatial relations are my thing. Sometimes I don't feel as if I need to measure when I'm building, but I do, because materials are expensive. I love it when things fit together, like those logs for the cabin."

"And you and Damon."

"For now, but I fully expect him to head back to California and put me out of his mind."

"Because he's figured out a system that chases away the bogeyman, and he's afraid to give it up."

Phil blew out a breath of frustration. "At this point I don't know what his bogeyman looks like."

"I'm no psychologist, but I think every trashed house he fixes up is his way of rewriting history. It's a pattern that works for him."

"Apparently so. He keeps saying how much he loves his life."

"I've heard him say that, too." Lexi paused. "But I've also seen how he looks at you. I'm not so sure he'll be

happy with it now. I hope he isn't. He's on a treadmill—
running like crazy but not going anywhere."

"Hey, where's my lady?" Cade's question filtered in
from the kitchen. "Rosie, have you seen Lexi and Phil?"

"Yep." Rosie's voice was pitched a little louder than
necessary, no doubt as a warning that the guys were on
their way. "They're trying to fit all that extra food in
the rec room fridge."

"Oh. Okay. We'll go find them." That announce-
ment was followed by the sound of booted feet on the
kitchen floor.

Phil walked over to the refrigerator, opened the door
and shoved one container a little deeper into its desig-
nated space, which made the adjacent ones rattle. "I
think that about does it!"

"Great job." Lexi came to stand behind her to complete the impression they were just finishing.

"Hey, there you are." Cade walked through the door
followed by Damon. "Thought you'd be in the kitchen."

Lexi gestured toward the refrigerator. "I was observing an artist at work. That woman knows her spatial relations."

Damon smiled at Phil. "She sure does. Those windows went in slick as a whistle today."

"Thank you." It truly was refreshing to have a man
appreciate her skill instead of dismissing her abilities.

"So, have you guys finished your beer?" Lexi went
over and slipped her arm around Cade's waist.

"We have." Cade pulled her against his hip and
nudged his hat back with his thumb as he gazed down
at her with slightly boozy devotion. "I was thinking you
and I might head out."

"That's fine with me. Are many people left out there?"

"Hardly anybody." Cade looked over at Phil. "In other words, the coast is clear."

"Okay." She blessed the dim light because she could feel herself blushing. "Guess I'll leave, too, then."

"I'll walk you out," Damon said.

Cade rolled his eyes. "It's just us chickens, genius. You don't need a cover story. Plus Rosie's the only one left in the kitchen. Everybody's headed home or to the fireworks. Nobody's going to question your behavior if you march out there and climb into Phil's truck."

"I think it's sweet that he's worried about my reputation." Phil was feeling protective. She didn't have all the facts about Damon's life, but it certainly hadn't been a bed of roses.

"Oh, me, too," Cade said. "Except it's a waste of energy in this case. You two can engineer it any way that feels right, but Lexi and I are riding on out of here. See you two in the morning." He guided Lexi through the door into the kitchen.

"We'll be on the job at dawn, Gallagher," Damon called after them. "How about you?"

"Might be a tad later than that, Harrison."

After they left, Damon looked over at her and held out his hand. "Come on, Philomena." His voice softened. "Let's go try out your sleigh bed."

"Okay." Her throat tightened as she put her hand in his. His grip was firm and strong. Somehow he'd managed to overcome whatever roadblocks had been put in his way and make a life for himself. What right did she have to mess with that?

They said good-night to Rosie as they walked through

the kitchen. She didn't try to delay them with small talk, and for that Phil was grateful.

She'd left her purse in her truck and the keys under the seat, as Damon had noticed and commented on this afternoon. He handed her up to the driver's side, and she moved her purse behind her seat as he rounded the hood and climbed in beside her.

He glanced at her and smiled. "Déjà vu all over again, huh?"

"Except this time we're really going to my house." She started the engine.

"My cabin's closer."

"Yes, but Ty and Brant are staying in Cabin Three."

"I know. I was kidding. Let's get out of here."

She put the truck in gear and had gone about ten feet when she put on the brakes. "Condoms. I left mine in your cabin, and unless you—"

"Put the box under the seat of your truck? You think I'd do something like that?"

She laughed and started off again. "I should have known."

"Hey, if you don't want people dumping condoms in your truck you should lock it. Oh, wait, that won't work because you like putting your keys under the seat."

"You are so damned observant it's scary."

"You learn to be when you're fighting for your life."

"I'm sure." She gripped the wheel and wondered if he'd confide any more.

"I haven't told you the particulars and I don't plan to. You'll have to trust me that I know what I need in my life. And that's what I've created for myself."

"I respect that."

"I hope so, because I'm being as honest with you as I know how."

"I appreciate that." If he didn't want to talk about his past, she'd honor his wishes. Her sleigh bed was waiting with clean sheets and the bedside lamp turned to a romantically low beam. "So let's talk about something else, like the rec hall Lexi and I think needs to be built."

"A rec hall." He settled back in the seat. "Now there's a concept."

"The rec room is too small for the group we're hoping to attract. And the academy probably will need some classroom space."

"Yeah, yeah, you're right. Now that I think about it, I can't imagine the rec room filled with sixteen hormonal kids. I remember what I was like at that age."

"And what were you like?"

He laughed. "I could say I was completely focused on sex, but then you'd think I haven't changed at all."

"But you have. I'm the one who went on the fake hunt for my keys. If I hadn't done that, you'd have controlled yourself until tonight."

"That's true. You absolutely lured me in there, flipping your hair around and wiggling your hips as you walked away. No man with a pulse could have resisted that siren song."

"Would you believe I've never acted that way before in my life?"

He was quiet for a moment. "Yes, I can. We have some powerful chemistry going on here."

"Does that scare you?"

"Some."

"I could turn this truck around and take you back.

We don't have to spend the night together if you're worried about the consequences."

"I said I was scared. I didn't say I couldn't handle it." He turned to her. "How about you?"

She had no idea how she'd deal with their inevitable breakup. Although she wouldn't let it take her down, it might be very rough on her. But she gave the only answer she could, because she wanted him so desperately. "I can handle it."

13

THEY SPENT THE rest of the drive talking about the rec hall. Damon agreed it was the thing to do, and he and Phil were the logical ones to build it. And yet if he came back later this summer, they'd continue their affair. They wouldn't be able to help themselves.

He was already in deeper than he'd ever been with any woman. Another week or two with Phil would strengthen those bonds. He couldn't let her become essential to his life, but spending more time with her would make that a very dangerous possibility.

Philomena was sexy, smart, capable, talented, funny and creative, and…she had the power to ruin his life. If he had any sense he would have accepted her offer to turn the truck around. Apparently, he liked living on the edge.

Besides, the house would be amazing. He knew that without setting foot in it, because she was amazing, and she would have put her personal touch on everything. When he renovated a place, he made it gorgeous, but in a generic way. Putting a personal stamp on a house limited the number of potential buyers.

He was fine with that. He wasn't even sure what his personal stamp would look like. Working with quality materials in neutral colors, he presented buyers with a blank canvas they could transform to their own tastes.

This cabin of Phil's wouldn't be anything like that. Her choices would be everywhere, and because he liked her so much, he was bound to like what she'd chosen. A sleigh bed. He knew what they were, but he'd never slept in one—or made love in one.

Sleighs made him think of Santa Claus, who'd never paid him a visit until he'd moved to Thunder Mountain Ranch. Christmas wasn't a big deal to him these days, but maybe he should plan to come back to the ranch this December. Herb and Rosie would like that.

But he couldn't come back without seeing Phil. This situation made him appreciate why Cade had stayed away for five years. It had taken Rosie's apparent heart attack for Cade to overcome his reluctance to face the mess he'd made with Lexi.

"This is it." Phil turned into a driveway that angled sharply up to a log cabin on a wooded slope. Light glowed from the front windows, creating a postcard scene, but she had to gun the motor to make the climb.

"This is a seriously steep grade. What do you do when it snows?"

She laughed. "Park at the bottom and walk up. It's a hassle, but it's a factor that affected the price. The driveway and the sad condition of the cabin gave me bargaining power. It's the only way I could have afforded it."

"I'll bet you drive a hard bargain."

She parked in front of the cabin and turned off the motor. "Depends on who I'm bargaining with." She glanced at him. "With you I'd be a pushover."

He couldn't see her face very well in the darkness, but he knew how she'd look, her blue eyes soft and inviting, her lips slightly parted, her cheeks flushed. She wanted him and wasn't afraid to let him know. "Same here," he said softly.

"Let's go in." She unfastened her seat belt. "I'm like a kid at Christmas. I can't wait for you to see what I've done with the place."

He understood that kind of eagerness, but he wondered how it felt to have the same surroundings all the time. Even at the ranch, which he'd loved, he'd grown restless when things became too static. Helping the adults build Cabins Two and Three had helped, and he'd pitched in with the rec room addition, too.

He had to fish the box of condoms out from under the seat, so by the time he climbed the steps to her front porch, she was already fitting her key in the lock. She really was excited to show him her creation, and he was touched. "Great door."

"I know, right? I bought it at an auction for practically nothing."

"And a front porch swing. Never had one of those."

She paused to glance at the wooden swing mounded with colorful pillows. "Found it at a yard sale. I love sitting out here and listening to the crickets at night."

"I can hear crickets right this minute. Want to sit out here for a bit?" Sure, he had other plans, but they could make out a while on the swing first. He had a real hankering to do that, in fact. The swing looked very inviting.

"Maybe tomorrow night, cowboy. Tonight I want to show you my house, and then I want to show you my sleigh bed. After that I doubt you'll have the energy to stagger out to the porch." She plucked the condom box from his hand and shook it. "Savvy?"

He grinned. She was so damned cute. "Savvy."

With that she flung open the front door and stepped inside. "Ta-da!"

He followed her in. As he looked around, he gave a low whistle.

"So you like it?" Her voice quivered with happiness. "I knew you would."

"I don't just *like* it. I love it." He walked straight to the rock fireplace and ran his hand over the mantel, a plank of cedar with the bark left intact along the edge. The surface had been sanded until the finish was like satin under his palm. Whoever had created it had chosen to use oil instead of shellac, which brought out the aroma of the wood. He took an appreciative sniff.

"I made that."

He turned to her. "Wow."

She beamed with happiness. "So this is the living room. Not real big, but—"

"It's perfect." He began wandering around, touching the refinished furniture and absorbing the…what, energy? His California friends would say something like that. The room had energy. He'd always thought blues and greens were cool colors, but these seemed warm, somehow.

He had the urge to sprawl on the sofa and watch TV. "Remember when you emailed about going to watch your cop show?"

"Yeah, I do." She continued to smile at him.

"Now I can picture you doing that."

"The coffee table converts to dining table height so

I can eat meals out here if I want to. There's no dining room, and I like being near the fire, so I do that a lot."

"We could, too."

"Absolutely. I like to cook."

He gazed at her. "You cook, you build cabins and you restore furniture. Is there anything you aren't good at?"

"Tons of things. I'm not a very good dancer, and I can't sing worth a lick. I'm horrible at Scrabble and although I like to cook, I'm not into gourmet dishes with a long list of ingredients. I can paddle a kayak but I never learned how to swim."

"I could teach you to swim." The minute he said the words, he wanted them back. "Well, except we don't really have time."

"I know. It's okay."

She probably understood that he hadn't meant to offer swimming lessons. Gestures like that came from men who planned to stick around a while. But as he stood in this living room that was so her and listened to the list of things she didn't do, he realized not a single one of those mattered to him. She was everything he'd ever dreamed a woman could be.

Well, except for the swimming. He'd become really fond of that since he'd moved to California. Surfing, too. But she could learn. Give him a few days and he'd have her churning through the waves like a pro.

But he wouldn't have a few days to teach Phil how to swim or surf. Why even think about such a stupid idea? Because he couldn't seem to help himself. She inspired him to imagine all kinds of scenarios that didn't fit with the life he had now. And the life he had now was the one that worked for him, that gave him what he needed and kept the demons at bay...mostly.

"Now onto the kitchen. I refinished all the cabinets."

"I'll just bet you did." He followed her into a kitchen with a mix of old and new appliances, something he'd never do in a house he was renovating to sell. But it worked here because this kitchen had something his always lacked—charm.

"The cabinets look terrific." He opened a door here, a drawer there. The hinges were smooth, and the drawers glided easily. He wasn't much of a cook, but he could understand why anyone who was would be excited to work in this space. The layout was efficient, and she'd used the cabinets and drawers the way he would if he ever had his own kitchen.

"I had to go with Formica instead of granite for the countertops as a cost-cutting measure. I may change that eventually."

He glanced up. "So this isn't all set the way it'll stay?"

"Heavens, no. I want a different light fixture in here, a chandelier of some kind, but I haven't found what I want yet. And I'm not sure about the finish on the cabinets. It may be too dark."

"You'd redo them?" That boggled his mind.

"I will if it starts to bother me. And besides, I like changing things around. I may refinish the living room floor and stain it a little darker. I'm trying to decide if I want a screen on the front door. It'd give me a breeze but I don't want to ruin the look of the door."

"I know a company in California that does amazing things with screen doors. You can check the website and see what they have, but they'll also customize one for you."

"Pricey?"

"Yeah, but I get a discount, so I—" He stared at her for a long moment. "What am I doing?"

"Confusing me, that's for sure."

He scrubbed a hand over his face and sighed. "Your house is great, and I got caught up in the moment. Sorry."

"I suppose we have to talk about what happens after this week, though. If we're going to put up that rec hall, we'll be working together again."

"True." He took a deep breath. This was getting more complicated by the minute. "I'm gonna want to be with you, Philomena."

"I'm gonna want to be with you, Damon."

"Can you accept the same parameters we have now? Lots of sex but no commitment?"

"As opposed to what? If I don't accept those conditions, then I'll be working with you all day and going home to my lonely bed every night. That doesn't sound like much fun to me."

He smiled. "Not to me, either. And speaking of that lonely bed, are you ready to show it to me?"

"Well, I *was* planning to give you a tour of the pantry and the coat closet and the—"

"Later." Grabbing her around the waist, he pulled her close. "Unless you had plans to seduce me in the pantry or the coat closet." He'd been aware of a mild but persistent ache in his groin, but he'd ignored it so he could pay proper attention to her house. Now that her soft body was nestled against the source of that ache, ignoring it was no longer an option.

"I'll tuck that idea away for another time." She tossed the condom box on the counter and slid both hands up his chest, massaging as she went. "After we've explored all the options of my sleigh bed."

"Mmm." Leaning down, he settled his mouth over hers. Ah. His tongue found its way between her parted lips, and he shifted his angle so he could go deeper.

She moaned, her fingertips pressing, stroking. His cock responded with an eager twitch. The memory of the way she'd licked the drops of sweat from his chest earlier today would stay with him forever, and it taunted him now.

He lifted his mouth a fraction away from hers. "Got any wood for me to chop?"

"What?"

"I'm not sweaty enough, but if I could swing an ax for twenty minutes or so, then—"

"Silly man," she murmured, capturing his hand and placing it over her left breast. "Feel my heart?"

He flexed his fingers, relishing the sensation of touching her there. All evening long he'd watched her and imagined how it would feel to hold her again, to feel her heart hammering against his palm. He grasped a fistful of the cotton T-shirt. "This needs to come off."

She lifted her arms as he pulled it over her head. "But now we don't match."

"We will in a minute." He tossed the shirt on the kitchen counter and started on the buttons of her blouse.

She leaned back to give him access. "We're not doing it in the kitchen."

He laughed and kept unbuttoning. "You sure are focused on that sleigh bed."

"You will be, too, when you see it." She rotated her hips against his.

He drew in a sharp breath at the tantalizing pressure

she'd just put on his swollen cock. "I will." He pulled the blouse from the waistband of her jeans. "But the contractor in me wants to test the strength of your counters." And he lifted her up on the nearest one.

"Damon…"

"Shh." He slipped the blouse from her shoulders and unfastened her bra. "I wanted to do this today, but there was no time. Now we have time."

"But—"

"Before we dive into that sleigh bed and I lose what's left of my mind, I want to see you, taste you…" He forgot what else he'd meant to say as he pulled off her bra.

This afternoon in the sunlight he'd thought of cinnamon, but tonight in her cozy kitchen he was reminded of eggnog sprinkled with nutmeg. She would be a thousand times sweeter.

Cupping his hands, he cradled her soft, pliant breasts and leaned down. Her nipples tightened under his gaze, and a shudder rippled through her body. "I think you like this," he murmured.

"Maybe." She gasped as he flicked his tongue against one rigid nipple. "But we're not—"

"Doing it here. I promise. We're only doing this." He began to lick and nibble the most tempting breasts he'd ever had the pleasure of tasting. The spicy scent of her skin matched its silky texture, and he was in heaven.

When he drew one nipple into his mouth, she whimpered. Hollowing his cheeks, he tugged gently. When she held the back of his head and arched her back, he knew her protests were over.

He left one breast damp and quivering while he paid equal attention to the other. She was luscious, a sensual treat that strained the bounds of his control. But he'd promised her the sleigh bed.

She moaned and shifted restlessly on the counter. As her breathing quickened, she abandoned her grip on his head and unfastened her jeans. "Please..."

Excitement fizzed in his veins. Change of plans. Scooting her close to the edge, he stripped off her boots, jeans and panties in no time. Then he dropped to his knees, propped her quivering thighs on his shoulders and found paradise waiting for him.

In the privacy of her house, she could cry out when he gave her pleasure. He rejoiced in the sounds she made as she urged him on, once again holding his head right where she wanted it. She came quickly, easily. He was ready to start over, but her grip tightened.

"The sleigh bed." Her order was breathless but clear.

"You bet." He scooped her off the counter. "Which way?"

"Through there." She pointed to a door down a short hallway.

He carried her there, and even though he was running hot on adrenaline and lust, he appreciated the grace and style of her bed. And the glorious expanse of that king-size mattress. They would do well here.

He laid her down. "Be right back." By the time he'd returned with the condoms, she'd shoved the blue-and-green-patterned quilt to the foot of the bed and lay waiting for him on sheets the color of the ocean on a sunny day.

He'd never undressed so fast in his life. He might have set a world record rolling on the condom. He didn't dive into her bed, although he wanted to. It might be an antique, and he didn't want to break it.

Instead he slid onto the mattress as if slipping beneath the waves. Moving over her, he looked into her beautiful eyes, and buried his aching cock in her luxurious heat. Restraint was out of the question. He plunged into her again and again as their mingled cries filled the small bedroom.

He maintained a sliver of control, one that allowed him to wait until he felt the first squeeze of her climax. After that, it was no holds barred. He drove into her with enough force to lift her off the mattress and make the bed squeak. When she came, she yelled, and when he came, he probably rattled the rafters. It was that good.

They collapsed into a heap afterward, but he managed to adjust his position so most of his weight wasn't resting on her. She was sturdy, but that didn't mean he could give her all two hundred pounds of him. She murmured something, but the blood was still singing in his ears, and he couldn't make it out.

He lifted his head and glanced over at her. "I didn't catch that."

"I said thank you."

Chuckling, he eased away from her and climbed out of bed to dispose of the condom. "Oh, no. I'm the one who should be thanking you. That was incredible."

"It was." There was a smile in her voice. "And it's exactly how I imagined sex could be in this sleigh bed."

"Exactly? How so?" he called from her bathroom. The cabinets looked great.

"I envisioned that we'd be wild for each other."

"Which we were. Are. As soon as I recover." He returned to the bed and stretched out beside her. "What else did you imagine about this scene? Wait. Don't tell me." He propped his head on his hand so he could look at her. "A handsome contractor with gray eyes and strong muscles."

"Sorry." She gave him a teasing glance. "I didn't get that specific."

"Damn it."

"But you, or whoever it was, would be on top, at least the first time."

The thought of someone else in this sleigh bed with her really bothered him, but he'd get over it. He took note that next time they might want to flip the action. "I didn't think about it. I just acted on instinct."

"I could tell. That's what made it so special. There was nothing calculated about any of it. And we made the bed squeak."

"That was part of your vision?"

"I've always thought that really good sex should make the bed squeak if it's a beautiful old one like this."

"You're not worried that a squeaky bed is an unstable bed? One that will come apart in the middle of the action?"

"This one won't. It's antique, but it's solid. And a little noise from the wood makes it become part of the lovemaking somehow."

He reached over and combed his fingers through her glorious hair. "I'm almost afraid to admit this, but what you just said makes some kind of crazy sense to me. I've never thought of it that way, but I get it."

She smiled at him. "I knew you would. It's a carpenter thing."

As he looked into those incredible eyes, he understood the full extent to which he was screwed. He'd never allowed himself to fall for a woman. Until now.

14

A NIGHT WITH Damon in her sleigh bed had been everything Phil had hoped. They'd made love twice more then slept curled up together in the middle of the big mattress. They'd showered together in the early morning and he'd helped her cook breakfast before they'd driven to the ranch.

Someday she might wish she hadn't indulged that sleigh-bed fantasy with him, one that they'd no doubt repeat again each night he was here. She could come to regret going all in with this man because of the indelible memories he'd leave behind. But at the moment worrying seemed a waste.

She sat on the stoop of the new cabin waiting for Damon to change into his work clothes. They'd both decided she'd better not watch him get dressed and put the schedule in jeopardy. Instead she gazed at the light edging down the flanks of the Big Horn Mountains and listened to the birds waking up in the nearby pines.

Damon found her there and held out both hands to pull her to her feet and into his arms. His kiss was gentle, and he kept his embrace easy as he lifted his head to look into her eyes. "After last night, I'm not frantic anymore."

"Good." She wrapped her arms around his waist. "Me, either."

"I think it's knowing we'll be back in your sleigh bed tonight. If it's okay with you, I'll just bring my duffel so I'll have my work clothes there in the morning."

"Sure." One day at a time. Her dad had said that phrase so many times, and until now she'd never understood the value in it. She'd constantly been looking ahead, figuring out what would happen next week, next month, next year.

Today she'd enjoy satisfying work followed by a night of satisfying sex. If she could design a perfect day, it would be a lot like this one. And if she could design a perfect night, it would involve getting naked with Damon.

Awareness flickered in his gray eyes, and his arms tightened a fraction. "Okay, I'm not frantic, but I'm not dead. When you look at me like that, my resolutions go right down the drain."

She laughed and backed out of his embrace. "Then let's get to work. We have a cabin to build."

Working hard with only a short break for the lunch Rosie brought, they made good progress. They mounted ladders as they started framing the roof. She'd loved jungle gyms as a kid, and the roof was her favorite part of any project.

They had little need for communication as they climbed around the structure, getting it ready for the green-coated sheets of metal that would make it weatherproof. They were both perched on extension ladders using nail guns when Cade rode up on Hematite, his black gelding.

"Looking good!" he called out during a break in the racket. "It's past six o'clock. You gonna work until it gets dark or what?"

Damon glanced over at Phil. "We could stop here if you're ready."

"Sure, why not?"

"Then let's blow this taco stand." As he climbed down, he called over his shoulder to Cade. "Yeah, we're quitting. Don't go away. I want to ask you something."

"I'm not going anywhere. I rode over here to tell you that Lexi thinks the four of us oughta take Herb and Rosie into town for dinner at the Mexican restaurant we all like. Rosie especially needs a break from the kitchen."

"I can't speak for Damon," Phil said, "but I'm a grubby mess, and I don't have a change of clothes with me."

"I could use a shower." Damon glanced over at Cade. "How about giving us a head start so we can get cleaned up at Phil's house? Then we'll meet you at the restaurant."

Cade grinned. "Okay, but text me if you get unavoidably delayed."

"We'll be there on time, smart-ass. By the way, did you make that phone call?"

"I did. I'll tell you all about it at dinner."

"Great. Can't wait to hear about it."

"It was...exciting." Cade touched the brim of his hat. "See you guys at the restaurant." He turned his horse around and trotted toward the barn.

At that moment Damon envied Cade, who was living

the kind of ranching life they'd cherished as teenagers. Then he pushed the thought away and looked over at Phil. "Last night he promised me he'd call the Chance family today."

"Wow. That's big news."

"I know. Important news. I'm glad he came over here because I got so involved with, well…everything, that I forgot I wanted to ask him about it. He has a tendency to procrastinate if something's going to be uncomfortable for him."

"I know. I heard all about it from Lexi before I ever met him. I wasn't prepared to like him very much, but it turns out I like him a lot."

"So do I, and I know what it must have cost him to make that call. I need to buy him a drink, for starters, because that was a huge step for him. I also want to find out what happened. I know we'd planned to have dinner at your house, but—"

"No worries. There's always tomorrow night." But as she and Damon took down the ladders and put away the tools, she did a quick count of the opportunities to cook for him.

She couldn't deprive Rosie and Herb of sharing a meal with him on the last night before he went back. Yes, he'd probably come home with her later, but that wouldn't be the same as relaxing over a meal and spending time on the front porch. Tomorrow night was the only time she'd be able to make dinner. She was a little shocked to realize they were almost at the end of his visit.

She finished putting the tools away while Damon went to get his duffel and repacked whatever he'd taken out of it. She finished before he did, so she paced in front of his cabin while she tried to get back the mellowness from this morning.

Carrying his duffel, Damon walked out of his cabin and paused. "You're okay with going to dinner, I hope?"

"Of course!" She stopped pacing. "Rosie deserves a night out, and I want to hear about Cade's phone call, too. We'll do what we'd planned tomorrow night. No problem."

He walked over and cupped her cheek with his free hand. "You didn't look very happy when I first came out."

She held his strong hand against her face. His touch felt so good. "I was just doing a little reality check and realized how soon you'd be leaving. Two nights of having dinner at my house seemed like a lot, but one night doesn't seem like enough."

"I know." He stroked his thumb over her cheekbone.

"We need to go have dinner with everyone, though. So we will, and we can sit on the porch swing for a little while when we get back."

"I'd like that. Sorry the shower will be a rushed deal."

"It's fine." Turning her head, she kissed his palm. "We'd better get going."

"Right." He laced his fingers through hers and they walked hand in hand to her truck. Soon they were headed down the road toward town.

Time was running out, but she had him with her now. Only a fool would waste these moments with thoughts of his imminent departure. She looked over at him. "If this is prying, you can tell me to mind my own business, but I'm really curious about the blood-brother situation."

He gave her a soft smile. "What do you want to know?"

"Did you cut your hands and mingle your blood like you read about in books?"

"Yep."

"Huh." She couldn't imagine doing that, but then it was probably more of a boy's thing. "How old were you?"

"Cade and I were thirteen, and Finn was still twelve. It was Cade's idea, although I latched on to it pretty quick. But when it came to slicing my hand with his pocket knife, I got sick to my stomach. Couldn't do it. Embarrassing as hell."

"So then what?"

"Cade did it for me. He and I are probably the only two people who know that. He's pretty damn loyal. And now you know."

"I won't tell." She sped up a little. She'd been engrossed in the story and had slowed until she wasn't even doing the speed limit.

"It doesn't matter now, but it's one of those things I remember about Cade. He could have told Finn but he didn't."

"Wasn't Finn there?"

"No, he wasn't even invited. He was new, and we didn't know if we liked him yet. He heard us sneak out into the woods in the middle of the night and followed us. We felt sorry for him and let him be a blood brother. He cut his own hand without hesitation. He had cojones."

"What about the other foster boys? Didn't any of them want to be blood brothers, too?"

"Of course. But at the time we were the only three at the ranch, and when the others came in, one by one, we thought it was cool to be exclusive. We said the Brotherhood was this special thing because we were the first three Rosie brought to the ranch. We kind of implied she liked us better."

"I can tell you right now that she does. She keeps saying she shouldn't have favorites, but you three are definitely her favorites. You should hear her brag." *Especially when she's trying to fix me up with you.*

"It's probably best if I don't hear that. Anyway, I think she's not particularly fond of me at the moment."

"Yes, she is. That woman has an enormous capacity for unconditional love. No matter what you or anyone else she's taken in does she'll love you forever. I'm no expert, but I think that's kind of rare."

"I know it is. I feel the same about her. And Herb, too. I've let too much time go by between visits, but I plan to fix that."

"She thinks you didn't come back very often because you needed to establish your independence."

He glanced at her. "She said that?"

"Yes, and I related to it because that's why I moved to Sheridan. I didn't go as far from my dad as you did from Rosie and Herb, but I was feeling way too dependent on him."

"It's good to know that you can make it on your own."

"Definitely." She'd need every ounce of that independent spirit when he left. She would have to remind herself why he'd moved away and why he'd chosen to stay in California. "We'd better plan out the shower schedule so we can go zip, zip, once we get in."

"You can have first shower."

"While you do what?"

"Go crazy thinking about you naked, what else?"

"I guess we'd better not shower together."

"No, and I'd planned on that, too. But unless we want to end up strolling into the restaurant when everyone's having dessert, we'll have to shower separately."

"Doesn't sound like much fun."

"Do you have an alternative, Philomena?"

"I might. But we have to work fast."

"I can work really fast, especially when I'm already getting hard thinking about shower sex."

Excitement curled in her belly. "Then here's the plan. Strip off our clothes on the way to the bathroom. Leave them as they lay. Climb in the shower, give each other a quick orgasm, and hop back out. I'll bet we can get to the restaurant long before dessert."

"I'm so in."

"We can't dawdle. Later on tonight, we can dawdle, but this has to be speedy sex. It might not be the best time we've ever had, but we won't sit through dinner feeling frustrated."

He laughed. "I love how you think."

"Good." She gunned the motor to make it up the driveway. "Because the race is on." Switching off the engine, she jumped down from the truck and ran up the steps with Damon right behind her. She unlocked the door and made a beeline for the bathroom, shedding clothes as she went.

Turning on the water, she flung off the last of her clothes before stepping into the shower. During her renovation she'd ditched the tub in order to create a walk-in shower, which she preferred. It wasn't huge, but that made it all the cozier when he stepped in behind her.

Moving under the spray, she doused herself thoroughly with water before turning around. "Ready?"

He smiled and gestured toward his cock, which stood at attention.

"Perfect." She started to kneel in front of him but he grasped her arms and pulled her back up.

"Ladies first," he murmured.

"Uh-uh. And we don't have time to argue."

"But—"

"Be quiet, Damon." She eased out of his grip and sank to her knees under the pelting water. Then she wrapped her fingers around that bad boy and began to stroke its rigid length.

"Not likely if you keep that up."

"I mean, just let me." And she took him into her mouth.

His sharp intake of breath was gratifying, as was his shudder of reaction when she began using her tongue. He'd come fast, and considering how this was affecting her, so would she. When she raked him gently with her teeth, he quivered so much he was forced to brace one hand against the tiled wall for support.

Gripping the base of his shaft with one hand, she cupped his balls with the other and started a slow massage. One swift move and she took him all the way to the back of her throat. Then she eased up again and applied intense suction to the very tip.

He groaned as she stroked the sensitive spot behind his balls. At last she took all of him in once more and sucked hard. He came with a bellow of satisfaction that filled the tiny bathroom. She swallowed everything he gave her before drawing back.

With surprising strength considering the way he'd trembled during his climax, he pulled her to her feet and claimed her mouth. She nestled her slick body against his and sucked on his tongue as he thrust it deep. Backing against the shower wall, he leaned against it as he turned her around and pulled her in close.

As he cradled her breasts, she arched into his palms with a soft whimper. Slipping one hand between her thighs, he combed his fingers through her wet curls, seeking…there. He pushed deep and began loving her as his cock, which should be napping, thickened. Nothing to be done about that. He stroked faster and rotated his thumb over her clit. She moaned and shook in his arms.

He put his mouth next to her ear. "Come for me, Philomena. Let go."

She tensed as her orgasm edged nearer.

"That's it. Take what you need." He pumped his fingers faster, and she gasped out his name.

Then the dam broke, and she came with a wail of pure pleasure. He stayed with her. She sagged against him, sated, but as he continued to caress and explore, the urgency returned. He stroked her breasts, her belly, her bottom, everything he could reach. She felt so wet, so sexy, so ready for more.

His breath was hot in her ear. "I want you again."

Her response came between quick breaths. "I want you again, too."

"Not here." He released her long enough to shut off the water. Then he helped her out and grabbed a towel, but neither of them bothered to use it. Uttering a soft oath, he scooped her up and carried her into the bedroom, where they tumbled down on top of the comforter.

She hadn't turned lights on before they'd left this morning, so they had nothing except what spilled through the bathroom doorway. That was better. This wasn't about slow and tender.

There was nothing relaxed about the way they grappled and rolled on the bed, their bodies still wet, their mouths hot and eager for the taste of each other. She took his cock in her mouth again, but he stopped her before she could make him come.

Wrenching open the nightstand drawer, he grabbed one of the condoms they'd stashed there. By the time he had it on, she'd rolled onto her back, parted her thighs and bent her knees.

A wild woman had taken command of her senses, and she barely recognized her own voice. "Come and get what you want, cowboy."

He moved over her and thrust with enough momentum to slam the headboard against the wall.

"Yeah." Her laughter was low and breathless. "Like that."

"You got it." He pumped hard, and that headboard banged into the wall every time.

She dug her fingers into his butt. *"More."*

He gave her more, and the headboard hit the wall faster and faster. Even though she hadn't worried about whether she'd have an orgasm this time, she did, anyway, hollering like crazy. He followed right on her heels, his cries drowning out hers. Dear God. The climax of the century. She thought the top of her head would come off.

He was still breathing hard when he levered himself up to gaze at her in the dim light. "Wanna skip dinner?"

She grinned. "You know I do."

"Great. Let's—"

"But we won't." She slapped him firmly on his delicious ass. "Move it, cowboy. We have people to see."

Operating as quickly and efficiently as they did on the construction site, they got dressed in record time.

As they started out the door of her house, he paused to survey the trail of clothes that led to her bathroom. "We made quite a mess. And your bed's a wreck."

She remembered his need for order. Leaving her house trashed might really bother him. "I know. But if we take time to pick up—"

"Hell, I wasn't about to suggest that." He smiled. "To tell you the truth, if creating a disaster zone leads to that kind of sex, I'm all for it."

She returned his smile. "Good to know." They were so much in tune. It was easy to imagine he could be happy staying in Wyoming. But he wouldn't be. He'd made that clear, and she'd support his wish to keep some distance from Thunder Mountain Ranch…and from her.

15

THE OTHERS WERE being served their meals by the time Damon and Phil arrived, so naturally they had to endure some teasing comments. Damon didn't care. That wild interlude with Phil had been the most carefree sex he'd ever had, especially tumbling into bed still wet from the shower.

When he thought of the soaked comforter and pillows, not to mention the clothes scattered throughout her house, he didn't cringe and wish they'd cleaned it up. Instead he remembered how she'd abandoned herself to the experience. And to him.

No woman had ever done that before, but it might be partly his fault. If they'd sensed his need for order, they might not have dared. Apparently, he didn't intimidate Phil at all, which made him smile.

He was grateful for her sense of adventure. The comforter and pillows would dry, and the clothes would be gathered up. But the memory of their crazy, spontaneous lovemaking would stay with him forever.

After Damon and Phil's orders had been taken, Rosie nudged Cade, who was sitting next to her at the round table. "Okay, they're finally here, so you can tell us about the phone call." She glanced at Damon. "He wouldn't say a word until you arrived."

Cade put down his goldfish bowl of a margarita. "Didn't want to have to repeat myself."

Damon felt a twinge of guilt for thinking earlier that he and Phil could have skipped this dinner. Good thing she'd insisted. He focused on Cade. "Thanks for waiting for me, bro. So what happened?"

"Well, I called the number Molly gave me."

"Yeah, yeah." Rosie made a rolling motion with one hand. "Cut to the chase."

"I asked for Jack Chance."

"Did you get him?" Like everyone in northern Wyoming, Damon had heard of the fabled Chance family and the historic Last Chance Ranch. Jack was the eldest son, and after his father's death several years ago, he'd become the acknowledged leader of the clan.

"I didn't get him right away, but I talked to his mother while somebody went to fetch him."

"That would be your Aunt Sarah," Lexi said.

Cade exchanged a look with her. "I suppose she is, but I didn't call her that." He shrugged and took another swallow of his margarita. "Maybe eventually that won't feel weird and I can do it. Anyway, she must have been able to tell I was nervous as hell, because she was so kind. Then Jack came on the line, and I don't know how to explain this, but we seemed to... I don't know...recognize something in each other. Does that make sense?"

"It does to me," Rosie said. "Molly's hinted that Jack didn't have an easy childhood, and his dad's death hit him hard."

"Molly's mentioned that to me, too. But even if she

hadn't, something in his voice was familiar, as if he understood things about me because he'd been there." He looked across the table at Damon. "You'd hear it. Any of us would."

"So you told him about Thunder Mountain Academy?" Damon leaned forward, eager for the news.

"I did. Gave him all the basic info. We'll talk more about it when Lexi and I go over there this month, but Dominique will call me tomorrow about the calendar. He's positive she'll love the concept. *He* loves the concept. He wanted to know if he could become an honorary part of the group so he could be in it."

Damon laughed. "Hell, he can have my month."

"Nice try, amigo." Cade shook his head. "But adding Jack doesn't mean we subtract you."

"Yeah, I know. In any case, congratulations. And I'm paying for that ginormous margarita, too."

"As a matter of fact, you are." Cade looked pleased with himself. "When I ordered it, I told our server to put it on your bill whenever you showed up."

"Fine with me. You earned it." Damon stood and reached across the table for their ritual handshake. "Great job."

"Thanks." Cade's eyes glowed with pride as he shook Damon's hand and met his gaze.

It was a moment Damon wouldn't have wanted to miss, not even for an uninterrupted night in Phil's bed. After he sat down, he lowered his voice to a pitch he hoped only she could hear. "Thank you."

"You're welcome."

"Hey, you two." Cade grinned at them. "Enough with the sweet nothings. You can pick up where you left off when you get back to Phil's house."

"Leave them alone," Rosie said. "I think it's lovely that they're getting along so well."

"Me, too." Lexi winked at him. "Worked out okay after all, didn't it, Damon?"

"Yes, it did." Under the table he reached for Phil's hand and gave it a squeeze.

Rosie beamed at them. "It does my heart good to see the two of you looking so happy."

Cade lifted his margarita in their direction. "I'll drink to that. Anything that does Mom's heart good is a plus in my book. Props to you guys."

"It seems a shame that you're leaving so soon, though, Damon," Rosie said.

"Have to." He didn't like thinking about it, either. "I promised my buyer the house would be ready in two weeks."

"All right." Rosie obviously wasn't deterred. "So you have to take care of that, but after you're done, why not drive back over and stay for a while?" She turned her attention to Phil as if seeking an ally. "Wouldn't that be nice?"

Phil hesitated. "Um, actually—"

"I'd be in favor," Cade said. "Lexi's convinced me that we need a rec hall, and if you and Phil could finish it this summer, before we have to worry about bad weather, that would be terrific. I realize that keeps you from starting on another house in California, but I think we can squeeze out some money to compensate you. Phil, too, for that matter."

Herb spoke up. "Definitely. The rec hall will take longer than the cabin, and we can't ask either of you to work without pay. We padded the Kickstarter amount a little for situations just like this, so I think we can swing it if you can wait until September first for the money."

Damon was torn. The prospect of coming back in a couple of weeks and spending more time with Phil was way too appealing. He wanted to help build the rec hall, but putting it up this summer wasn't critical.

By postponing the project until spring, he'd have months to settle into his regular routine before seeing her. A long break was probably a wiser course of action if he wanted to keep their connection low-key. Ha. It had never been low-key.

That might be even more reason to nix the idea of driving back here this summer. They both could use a cooling-off period. He couldn't very well explain that to everyone at the table, though. He wasn't even sure that he wanted to.

The idea of coming back in two weeks hovered in his imagination, a tantalizing image of hot, sweaty days and passion-filled nights with Phil. He had to believe she was thinking the same thing. When she gave his hand a squeeze under the table, he was sure of it.

Then she slipped her hand free and cleared her throat. "I think we need to let Damon get back to his work in California rather than expecting him to make another trip over here so soon."

He stared at her in astonishment. That was the last thing he'd expected her to say.

She smiled at him before continuing. "He's been incredibly generous with his time and talents. I know he'll agree to do anything he can for the project, but if we wait until spring to put up the rec hall, he can schedule it in advance instead of dropping everything to build it now. He might not tell you it's inconvenient, but I suspect it is."

Herb nodded. "You make a good point. We don't want to impose on you, Damon."

"It's not an imposition. I've never thought of it that way. I'm glad to help out."

Rosie looked worried. "I don't want to impose, either. But I thought, since you and Phil work so well together, that…" She made a vague gesture with her hand. "You'd want to come back over this summer."

"Well, I—"

"Rosie." Phil's voice was gentle. "We get along great, as I'm sure you've figured out. But that doesn't mean we're a couple. Whether he comes back in two weeks or months from now makes no difference, either to me or to him."

No difference? That sure wasn't true for him, and he couldn't believe it was true for her, either.

Cade had been watching them both intently, and finally he took a deep breath and focused on Damon. "You know what, bro? Phil's right. We should let you get back to the job that brings in the money. No matter what we can scrape together, I doubt it'll equal what you'll earn doing your own thing. The rec hall can go up next spring, no problem."

Damn it, now he was irritated. "I'm not concerned about the money. And even if I don't come back in two weeks, I'll show up for Christmas. Can't do outside construction, but I can put in the bunks and the desks in the new cabin." Of course he'd have no excuse to see Phil then. For all he knew, she'd head down to Cheyenne to be with her father and stepmother.

"Excellent idea," Rosie said. "I'd love you to come

home for Christmas. I just hope we're still at—" She caught herself. "Sorry." Her jaw firmed. "Herb and I will be waiting at the ranch with bells on."

"Literally," Herb said. "Last year I got us each a Christmas sweatshirt with bells sewn on the front."

"Sounds great. Count on me." But whether he came back for the holidays or not wouldn't matter much to Phil, apparently. He'd thought for sure she'd want him to return this summer, but instead she was arguing in favor of his staying away. That stuck in his craw.

"I will plan on it, then." Rosie still looked worried, though, as if she sensed something wasn't quite right. "And by the way, the cabin is coming along beautifully."

"Thanks. We might be able to finish it tomorrow." He thought about his suggestion that he and Phil drag a mattress in there and spend the night as a celebration of what they'd accomplished together. Now he wondered if that would mean anything to her.

Their food arrived, and he ate because a hard day's work plus sex made him hungry, but he didn't feel nearly as warm and cozy as he had when they'd walked into the restaurant. Sure, Phil had accepted the limits on their relationship, but tonight she'd seemed almost clinical about it, as if she didn't care whether they spent time together or not. He hadn't expected that.

He didn't try to hold her hand under the table anymore, but he pretended everything was cool as they all said their goodbyes in the parking lot. Phil seemed to be cheerful enough.

But Rosie obviously knew something was wrong. She made a point of coming over to give him a hug. "I hope everything's okay."

"Everything's great, Mom." He hugged her back.

"I just—"

"Don't worry about it."

"All right." She patted his cheek. "I'll bring you guys lunch again tomorrow."

"Perfect. See you then."

Phil glanced over at him. "Ready?"

"Yep." Damn it, the last time she'd said it they'd been standing in her shower about to have sex. He wondered if that crossed her mind or if she'd forgotten all about it already.

As they walked to her truck, he knew he had to say something about the discussion in the restaurant. He couldn't just go back to her house, have more sex and not talk about it. Her attitude really bothered him.

She reached for the door handle, and he put a restraining hand on her arm. "Hang on a minute. I have a question."

She turned to face him. "About what?"

"How come you jumped right in and suggested I should head back to California and stay there?"

She studied him for a moment. "I don't believe I put it quite like that."

"Not word for word, but that was the general idea."

"Isn't that what you want?"

"Well, yeah, in a way, but...would you like me to come back this summer? Because if you would, I sure couldn't tell from the conversation."

She stared at him without speaking.

"I guess I have my answer, then. It's exactly like you said, that it doesn't matter one way or the other."

"What in hell are you talking about?"

"The fact that you don't seem to care whether I stay or go! That's what I'm talking about!"

"I can't believe you." Her voice was low and intense. "You laid it all out for me in the beginning. You said how important it was that you stay unattached so you can do your own thing. I thought you'd want to get back to California and live the way you seem to prefer!"

"I do, but being with you is great, too."

She blinked. "So you want me to ask you to stay? Is that it?"

"No. I know you wouldn't do that, especially in front of other people. But the way you reacted, it's as if you don't give a damn what I do."

"Of course I give a damn! But I'm honoring the parameters you set out. I'm following your guidelines."

"So you'd actually like me to come back in two weeks?"

She blew out a breath. "Do *you* want to come back in two weeks? Is that what this is all about?"

"Truthfully, it might be better if I didn't, but—"

"Damon, do you even know what you want?"

He gazed at her. She was so pretty right now. She'd managed to dry her hair in the short time they'd had, but it wasn't styled as carefully as usual. She looked mussed and frustrated and adorable. He wanted her, but that was only a partial answer to her question. He didn't have a complete answer.

"You really *don't* know what you want, do you?"

He sighed. "I guess not."

She was quiet for a moment, and when she spoke, her soft voice held a note of resignation. "Okay, here's the deal, cowboy. I can handle knowing you want to leave. I can handle knowing you want to stay. I can't handle not knowing if you want to leave or stay."

He swallowed the lump in his throat. "Fair enough."

"This will be a little awkward for both of us, but I'm going to drive you to my house so you can get your stuff. Then I'm taking you back to the ranch."

He couldn't very well argue with her about that. She'd respected his boundaries and now he needed to respect hers. "Okay."

The trip back to her house was blessedly short. Once there, he focused on locating all his stuff to avoid thinking about the incredible joy he'd found with her and that it was now over. She was right about him, so damned right. He was confused and didn't know what he wanted—at least not now, when she was so close and tempting.

He'd be fine once he got to California, though. She was probably right about that, too. She knew him better than he knew himself, so she was cutting the ties and urging him back into his comfort zone.

The ride back to the ranch was longer and excruciatingly silent. He questioned everything a thousand times during that endless trip. But now that he'd revealed his uncertainty there was no going back. She was smart to keep her distance, because in another two days he'd be gone. And he'd rediscover that his familiar routine was what he needed even more than he needed her.

But as she pulled up near the cabin, he remembered that they weren't finished with the job. So he had to ask. "Will you be here tomorrow?"

"Of course."

"You'll be able to work with me?"

She stared straight ahead. "Yes."

That's when he realized how strong she was. He'd suspected it all along, but here was tangible evidence. "Then I'll see you in the morning."

She glanced at him. "Will you be able to work with me?"

He met her gaze. "Yes. It will be my pleasure."

Her breath hitched. "See you tomorrow."

"Right." He grabbed his duffel and opened the passenger door. "Thanks for the ride."

"Sure thing."

He climbed down and shut the door. Then he watched her drive away. *Thanks for the ride*. It had been quite a ride, at that. Despite the way it was ending, he couldn't regret a single moment of it. Philomena Turner was not for him, but he'd never forget her.

16

DESPITE REPLACING THE wet comforter with a blanket and taking a dry pillow out of the closet, Phil slept like crap. Her throat hurt from the effort not to cry. She refused to give in to angry tears. Although she was furious, both with Damon and with herself, crying wouldn't accomplish anything except to give her puffy eyes in the morning. She wasn't about to show up at the job site like that.

But as she tossed and turned throughout the night, the image of that moment in the restaurant parking lot stayed with her. When she'd pounded the final nail in the coffin his face had lost all color. He'd said *fair enough*, but the bleakness in his gray eyes would haunt her forever.

Angry as she was, she still hated knowing that she'd hurt him. But there was no easy way to do this. A softer approach would have had them back in each other's arms pretending they could make it work for another couple of days.

Maybe he could have, but she was so done. This wasn't how she'd scripted the ending in her head. She'd imagined them parting with bittersweet smiles and some vague plans about handling his return in the spring. Instead they'd get through today and then never cross paths again.

She would scour the state for someone to take her place when he came back to build the rec hall. Between her connections and her dad's, she'd find someone competent. Maybe that person would have a teenager who'd like a tuition-free session at the academy. Somehow she'd make it happen.

When she drove down to the cabin at dawn the next morning, Damon was already attaching the green metal roof panels. From the look of things, he'd been at it for a while, which indicated he was as eager to get this job done as she was. She would almost believe he'd hooked up floodlights in order to work in the dark.

Damn, he looked good up there operating power tools. His biceps strained the sleeves of his T-shirt, and she was reminded of how easily he'd carried her to bed after they'd climbed out of the shower. Such a beautiful, confused man.

He paused and looked down at her, his smile tense. "Hey."

"Hey." She held his gaze for a moment and then looked away. Staring into those gray eyes was not good for her. "I'll be right up."

"Great." He went back to work.

They'd never required much communication in order to get the job done, so their lack of conversation throughout the morning wasn't any different from previous days. But the mood had totally changed. Twice they disagreed about how something should be done, and that hadn't ever happened before. He conceded to her both times.

They worked at a breakneck pace and had the roof on by midmorning. That left the ceiling insulation and the paneling that would cover it. Clouds moved in for the first time since the rain that had fallen the night before he'd arrived. The overcast sky seemed appropriate.

Rosie arrived right on schedule and seemed relieved to find them both inside the cabin putting up insulation. "Break time!" she called out in a cheery voice.

Phil had been dreading lunch, although she was hungry. Rosie liked to stay and chat while they ate, sitting on the benches Damon had brought over from the fire pit. Until now, the routine had been pleasant. Today it would be torture.

Predictably, Rosie exclaimed over what they'd accomplished since yesterday as she unpacked cold fried chicken and coleslaw with lemonade to drink and chocolate chip cookies for dessert. "Good thing the roof's on. We might get some rain today." She handed a plate of food along with a fork and napkin to Phil, who thanked her before glancing up at the sky.

"We might, at that."

"I'll bet you'll be finished by this afternoon, considering how close you are."

"We should be." Damon accepted his plate and thanked her.

"In that case, we need a celebration."

Phil almost choked on her food. She'd planned on leaving the minute they were done. She hadn't factored in a celebration to commemorate finishing the cabin, but she should have. That was typical of how the Padgetts operated.

"We'll bring one of the long folding tables down here with some chairs and set them up in the cabin, so we can eat, drink and admire at the same time. How's that?" Rosie looked expectantly at Damon and Phil.

"Sounds wonderful, Mom." Damon smiled at her. "Great idea."

"Yep." Phil nodded enthusiastically. "Terrific." She thought about Damon's plan to drag a mattress in there. Instead they'd have a family picnic that would require her to hang around when she longed to escape.

"I suppose you two will want to go back to Phil's house and clean up first, so just let me know when you're finished so I can organize the particulars."

Phil glanced at Damon, unsure of how to respond.

His gaze locked with hers for one intense moment as if signaling that she shouldn't say anything. Then he turned back to Rosie. "We'll let you know."

"This'll be fun." If Rosie noticed anything unusual in the way Phil and Damon were acting, she didn't let on. "I have some champagne tucked away for just this kind of occasion. I'll make sure Lexi and Cade can be there, and we'll all drink a toast to the fine job you two have done."

Damon's eyes flashed with humor. "Are you going to smash a bottle against the cabin?"

"Should I? I never thought of that!"

He chuckled. "I was kidding."

That soft chuckle tore at Phil's heart. His laughter was one of the most precious things about him. She would really miss it.

Rosie rolled her eyes. "I should have guessed you were pulling my leg. Who needs broken glass all over the place?"

"That reminds me," Damon said. "Does Dad still have that old shop vac? We'll want to clean up the area when we're finished."

"I think so. I'll ask him. If we do, it's in the tack room where it got used most. I can't think of that shop vac without remembering how you three boys used to pretend it was an alien life-form. As I recall, you even invented a language for it."

"You mean this?" Damon cupped his hands over his mouth and produced some garbled speech that sounded like a weird combination of Donald Duck and a power screwdriver.

Rosie and Phil started laughing. Phil didn't want to be charmed or entertained, but God, he was adorable. For a moment the tension was gone, but once Rosie left, it was back with a vengeance.

Damon's expression shut down. "She doesn't have to know yet," he said. "In fact, nobody really has to know anything, at least not tonight when Rosie's so set on celebrating."

"Don't you think they'll figure it out, especially if they notice that you don't leave with me?"

"If they do, they do, but I'd appreciate if you wouldn't say anything specific about our situation."

"I won't. I'll leave it all up to you."

"Thanks. Now we'd better get moving."

"Right."

Once again, they worked side by side without saying much of anything. They both knew what to do and so they did it with speed and efficiency. And then, far sooner than she would have expected, it was over.

Herb had brought them the famous shop vac, but if Phil had expected a demonstration of its alien personality, she didn't get it. While she put away their tools, Damon vacuumed up the construction dust. At last there was nothing more to be done.

They stood together outside the cabin, gazing at it during what should have been a triumphant moment. She had nothing to say, but she couldn't make herself just turn and leave, either.

"You're one hell of a builder," Damon said at last.

"You, too."

"The best I've ever worked with."

Her throat grew tight. "Same here."

"I guess that's it, then." He glanced over at her.

She met his gaze. "Guess so." Then she turned and walked back to her truck because if she stayed there a second longer, she was liable to do something she'd regret. She wasn't clear whether she'd tell him off or kiss him senseless. Maybe both. But neither was a good idea.

Without looking back, she knew he watched her go. She was pretty shaky as she started the truck and pulled away. Then, glancing in her rearview mirror, she saw Cade approaching Damon. So much for keeping the lid on things.

But when she returned after showering and putting on clean clothes, everyone was gathered around the cabin, and she'd never seen a jollier group. If they were concerned about the rift between her and Damon, they weren't showing it.

As she climbed from the truck, Cade called out to her. "Get a move on, Phil! You're part of the ribbon-cutting ceremony, and it's fixing to rain on us!"

Sure enough a yellow ribbon stretched across the doorway of the cabin, and she felt random raindrops on her skin. She'd bet Rosie had dreamed up the ribbon idea after the discussion about smashing a champagne bottle against an outside wall. Lexi snapped pictures of the cabin and the group gathered there.

Damon, dressed in a clean white Western shirt and his black dress jeans, held a large pair of shears in one hand. His shirt had a few little damp spots where rain had fallen on his shoulders. "We're supposed to do this together."

"Okay." She stepped close enough to get a grip on the scissors, too. It was the first time she'd touched him since he'd held her hand at the restaurant, and the feeling was so electric she was surprised sparks didn't fly.

This near to him, she caught the scent of his aftershave and noticed the change in his breathing as they stood there together. But despite her slight trembling and his unsteady breaths, they managed to make the ribbon-cutting look like a smooth joint venture, and the other four people cheered. Lexi recorded it all to put on the Kickstarter website.

"Everybody inside!" Herb made shooing motions as the rain pelted down faster.

Phil rushed in with everyone else, but once inside, she paused in astonishment. A white linen cloth had transformed the battered folding table into an elegant piece of dining furniture. A silver candelabra and white tapers would have provided atmosphere enough, but someone had put two low flower vases on either side of it. More vases sat on each of the four windowsills, and the chairs were decorated with big white bows.

The utensils gleamed, and the dishes were obviously Rosie's good china. Each plate was graced with an artfully folded cloth napkin. Two ice buckets holding uncorked champagne bottles sat on the table, and flutes were beside every place. A second linen-draped table off to the side had been reserved for the platters of food.

"Wow." Phil glanced at Rosie. "This is spectacularly beautiful."

"It wasn't just me," Rosie said. "Everybody helped."

That would have included Damon, so obviously they all knew she'd left without him this afternoon. Maybe he'd made up a reason and maybe not. It didn't matter. Soon they'd all realize the brief affair was over.

But that wasn't going to spoil this festive evening. She hadn't looked forward to spending more time with Damon, but seeing this effort made her determined to keep a positive frame of mind.

The champagne helped. Seeing Rosie and Herb looking hopeful about the future helped. Even Cade and Damon joking around with each other helped. In spite of a persistent ache near her heart, she had a darned good time.

The rain coming down outside made the cabin all the cozier, but by the time Phil had decided to drive home, it had stopped. "I should probably take advantage of the break in the weather to head out," she said, "but I don't want to leave you with all this to carry back up to the house. Can I take a few things before I go?"

"Nope." Herb stood. "We'll do it. You go ahead. Lexi and Cade might want to do the same. Damon, Rosie and I can bus the tables."

So there it was. Everyone knew about the change in circumstances and had decided to avoid any mention of it. She glanced over at Damon, who was also standing. "Then I'll see you all later."

His expression had become impassive again. "See you later, Phil."

And that would be their brief and inelegant good-bye. She looked into his eyes one last time. Awareness flickered there. For a moment she thought he might say something else.

"Come on, Phil," Lexi said. "We'll walk you out."

Chest tight and throat hurting, she left with Lexi and Cade.

As they approached her truck, avoiding the muddy spots along the way, Lexi spoke. "I have to drive Cade to the ranch tomorrow, but I don't have much going on after that, so let's do that first riding lesson."

"Thank you, but I don't think so."

"I do. I find it hard to believe you're booked since you just finished that cabin in record time."

"No, but I—"

"You should do it," Cade said. "Horses are the greatest therapists in the world."

"Look, guys, I appreciate the thought, but I'm not in the mood."

"You'll change your mind when you get out there." Lexi put an arm around her waist. "I'll pick you up at ten on my way back. We'll head over to the stables. I'll call them first to make sure they have Trigger available."

"Trigger?" Arguing with her seemed pointless, so maybe she'd just call her in the morning and cancel.

"Yeah, he's almost old enough to be the real Trigger! Just kidding. He's twenty-two and so gentle. You'll love him. See you then." Lexi gave her a quick hug. "Need us to follow you home?"

"No! I'm fine, really!"

"Okay. Tomorrow at ten." She and Cade headed over to her truck.

The storm held off until she made it home, and then it let loose again. She'd expected to spend another restless night, but the rain on her metal roof was one of her favorite sounds, and she slept well, so well that she decided to take that riding lesson after all.

She was ready at ten when Lexi pulled up. Grabbing her purse and Western hat, she walked out the door and locked it behind her.

"That's a hell of a driveway you have there," Lexi said as Phil got into the truck. "I didn't dare let up on the gas or I would have slid right back down."

"Deters burglars." Phil smiled at her. "Getting the U-Haul up here to empty the house is too much of a hassle."

"Good thinking." Lexi reached over and squeezed her arm. "How're you doing?"

"Not so bad." Especially if she didn't think about Damon.

"Soon you'll be even better." Lexi started the truck. "At least you have a circular drive so I don't have to back down at a forty-five-degree angle. I'll bet I can get up enough speed on this here exit ramp that I can coast all the way to the stables, no problemo."

Phil laughed. Maybe Lexi knew what she was doing, suggesting this horseback riding lesson. Phil was feeling better already.

A half hour into the lesson, Phil decided horses were her thing. Who knew? With Lexi's guidance, she'd practiced saddling and bridling Trigger, who was a big old lovebug who put up with her fumbling. Now she was riding him around the corral while Lexi called out things like *heels down, relax your lower back, chest up*.

Trigger was a really nice horse. His soft ears swiveled back whenever she praised his handsome gold coat and white stockings. He was such a great listener that she decided to tell him her troubles, and she had the feeling he understood and sympathized.

"Okay," Lexi sang out after another thirty minutes or so of circling the corral. "That's enough for today. We'll get that guy unsaddled, brush him down and go grab some lunch."

"Lunch? Hey, you don't have to babysit me."

"Who's babysitting? I was planning to let you buy." She grinned and took hold of Trigger's bridle to lead him back to the hitching post.

"In that case, how can I refuse?"

"That's the idea."

Later, as they sat in a well-worn booth eating hamburgers and drinking chocolate shakes, Phil glanced across the scarred table at Lexi. "You're good at this."

Lexi shrugged. "My friends took care of me when Cade left town. They made me go do stuff that first day or I would have chosen what I'll bet you had in mind—hiding out and feeling miserable."

"Did they take you riding?"

"No. For me, that would have been too ordinary, since I'm around horses all the time. There was a traveling carnival in town, and we rode the heck out of the Tilt-a-Whirl. I screamed until my throat was raw. It was great."

"Well, riding Trigger was perfect for me. You were right. He's better than a therapist's couch. I told him the whole story, and he didn't interrupt once."

Lexi's hazel eyes warmed. "So I take it you liked the experience?"

"I loved it. Let me know when you're available to do it again, and I'm so there."

"Tomorrow?"

"Seriously? Because I don't want you changing your plans just because I'm in sort of a crisis." But the thought of more Trigger time sounded wonderful.

"Isn't it great when life just works out? I have the next two days free. I recommend you take advantage of that."

"I will. Thank you." She could look forward to riding Trigger the day that Damon flew back to LA, too. Perfect.

17

SOMEHOW DAMON MADE it through the next day and a half before his flight left without borrowing a truck and driving over to Phil's house. He had a couple of close calls when the urge to see her nearly overwhelmed his better judgment, but he managed to control himself.

Back in California, his strategy was simple. He worked night and day on the house. The closing was in less than two weeks and the buyer was eager. Exhaustion was his friend, the only thing that allowed him to sleep when he finally fell into bed.

Unfortunately, he couldn't control his dreams. His nightmares seemed to have temporarily disappeared, which was the good news. Erotic fantasies involving Philomena had taken their place, which was the bad news. He'd wake up hot, sweaty and hard.

Sometimes he'd take a cold shower, and sometimes he'd surrender to the need for relief. But the dreams weren't his only reminder of her. He'd hear her voice in his head commenting on his work. She liked the base-boards but disapproved of the cream-colored walls. He found himself wanting to show her a ruler-straight grout line on his tile job.

For the first time he questioned all the neutral tones he'd used in the house. He went to the hardware store to pick up some finishing nails and ended up in the paint aisle examining swatches of blue and green while he considered using color in one of the bathrooms. When he realized what he was doing, he put the swatches back and left the store.

He'd been flipping houses long enough that he knew most people wanted to make those choices for themselves. He might hit it lucky and paint a room in a shade the buyer liked. More likely, though, he'd paint the bathroom the color of Philomena's eyes, and the buyer would prefer butterfly yellow.

Phil had gotten under his skin, no question about that. But once he experienced the thrill of turning the house over to the new owner, he'd be back in the groove. That special moment validated his way of life each time. It would do that for him again.

Finally, the day for the closing arrived. He'd packed his stuff into the construction trailer and taken it to storage. Normally, he had his next house lined up and was ready to move in and begin the process all over again. But the trip to Wyoming had thrown him off schedule, and so he'd rented a room in a suite hotel for a week until he got his act together.

He'd cleaned the house from top to bottom and on his final walk-through he'd been proud of what he'd accomplished. Phil might consider the house sterile, but he'd rather say it was sleek and sophisticated, ready for the buyer to make it his own.

The buyer was a single guy who wanted to surprise

his girlfriend with the purchase. Damon had his usual setup with the title company. They'd handle the paper-work, but he'd retain the keys and meet the guy at the house to hand them over. That was his ritual.

He had pictures on his phone of how the place had looked before he'd started working on it. He'd studied them again early this morning. As usual, they reminded him of the trashed apartments and duplexes he'd lived in as a kid. The buyer would never see those pictures, but Damon loved comparing them with the shots he'd taken after the work was finished.

The buyer and his girlfriend arrived right on time, and Damon turned over the keys. "I'd like to do a quick walk-through, in case there's anything that isn't the way you expected."

The buyer was an ambitious young executive type. "Sure thing."

The three of them entered a house filled with the scent of new wood and recently grouted tile. The house was clean, but it also smelled clean. The windows spar-kled, and the kitchen appliances gleamed.

The girlfriend went ballistic, and the guy winked at Damon. All was going as it was supposed to. They were thrilled, and any second now he'd feel the rush of accomplishment.

It didn't come. Instead he became absorbed in watch-ing the couple discuss how they would create a life together in this house. She talked about decorating schemes, and her boyfriend wrapped an arm around her waist as they surveyed the living room and dis-cussed furniture choices.

When Damon saw that simple gesture, he missed Phil so much he felt an actual stab of pain in his chest.

The realization came swiftly—he didn't want to be the contractor who'd transformed this house. He wanted to be part of a happy couple eager to move in. No, he didn't want that, either, because this house would never suit Phil.

Oh, she could fix it up with color and interesting furniture, but why would she? She had the house she wanted, the life she wanted. The next insight hit him so hard that he gasped out loud. She had the house and life *he* wanted, too.

He was in love with that house, but he was also deeply in love with Philomena Turner. Judging from the way he felt right now, that wasn't likely to change…ever. Because of that, everything else would have to change.

The girlfriend glanced at him in alarm. "Are you okay, Mr. Harrison? You look a little pale."

"Something I ate for breakfast." He managed a smile. "So, any questions?"

"Not that I can think of." Her boyfriend walked over and shook Damon's hand. "I have your card if anything comes up."

"Absolutely. I stand by my work." But they didn't need him hanging around anymore, so he wished them well and walked back out to his truck.

If everything had to change, he saw no reason to delay. The shift in his thinking seemed to be instantaneous, but he knew that wasn't true. It had started on the front porch of Thunder Mountain Ranch, the moment he'd looked into her eyes.

Before he climbed into his truck, he checked his wallet. He had a fair amount of cash and two credit cards. He'd gassed up early this morning. If he went to the hotel to grab his duffel, he could get delayed in LA traffic. If he left now from here, he could hit the 15 and be at Phil's house around 6:00 a.m.

Decision made. He'd have close to eighteen hours to figure out what he was going to say and how he was going to say it. Surely that would be enough time to come up with something brilliant.

A little over seventeen hours later, as he gunned the engine to climb Phil's ski slope of a driveway, he was still debating. He'd just have to wing it and hope she didn't throw him out. At least if she did he could head to the ranch.

She wouldn't throw him out, though. She'd had the guts to end their affair, but he knew it hadn't been easy for her. Chances were she still liked him well enough to listen to what he'd come here to say. And she should believe him. He'd never once lied to her.

He climbed the steps to her porch. Her little porch light illuminated the swing they'd never cuddled in. When they did cuddle there, and he was determined they would no matter how long it took to win her over, he'd want the porch light off.

Pulling out his phone, he checked the time. Not quite five. If she had a renovation job, she might be getting up about now. She started work at dawn if possible, just like he did.

But it wasn't dawn yet, and she didn't seem to be up—no water running, no lights shining through the front windows, no smell of coffee brewing. Her truck was here, though, so she hadn't gone anywhere.

Technically he should be tired, but adrenaline pumped through his system and made him jittery. Or maybe it was all the coffee he'd consumed during the trip. Because he hadn't wanted to look like a vagrant, he'd pulled into a truck stop a few miles down the road so he could shave and wash up.

He looked around for a doorbell and couldn't find one. Then he noticed something he'd missed before. She had a cast-iron door knocker instead. Simple. Old-fashioned. He never would have thought of that, but he loved the idea. Phil had good ideas.

After banging on the knocker, he stood and waited for a while. Nothing. He tried again, banging louder this time. That made him think of the way he'd banged her headboard against the wall that last night they'd made love.

He wondered if she'd had any second thoughts the next day. Guaranteed she'd have some dings in the wall and maybe the headboard. She might have repaired them so they wouldn't remind her of him. He remembered that she'd liked the squeaking of the bed frame, too. She'd been really cute about incorporating the bed into the experience.

God, how he loved her. He was fairly sure she loved him, although she was probably trying to get over it. He hoped she hadn't succeeded. He knocked again.

"Who's there?" Her voice was strong, challenging any intruder to think twice.

He imagined her standing in the living room with a fireplace poker in her hand, just in case. It made him smile. "It's me, Damon."

"No, it's not. Whoever you are, you'd better get out of here. I have a big dog."

"You do? Since when?"

"Damon?" The lock clicked, and she opened the door wearing the same caftan she'd had on the night she'd driven out to the ranch without underwear.

"Where's your dog?"

"I made that up to scare you. I mean, to scare the creep I thought was pretending to be you."

"I'm glad you're cautious." Man, she was beautiful. Her hair was all tousled, and the caftan shifted when she moved so he could see the outline of her breasts. "Then I guess I didn't ruin it."

"Ruin what?"

"Your caftan."

"No, it washed up okay. But what in hell are you doing here? What's the matter?"

He took a deep breath. "Nothing. Well, all kinds of things, but they can be fixed if… Listen, can I come in? It's been a long trip. Seventeen hours."

"Um, sure." She didn't have a fireplace poker in her hand, but she seemed a little tense as she stepped away from the door.

Not surprising. She'd ordered him out of her life for a good reason. He had a lot of explaining to do before she'd consider letting him back in.

He walked through the door, and she closed it behind him. Then she reached over and pulled the chain on a Tiffany-styled table lamp he'd especially liked the couple of times he'd been here.

He gazed at his surroundings as if seeing them for the first time. *Home.* Why hadn't he realized that before? He let out a sigh and turned to her. "I should probably make this prettier and more poetic, but I'm a tradesman, and I think in basic terms."

She swallowed. "What are you talking about?"

"My own stupidity, mostly." He spread his arms. "My blindness to what I've craved all my life. It was right here. You were right here."

"I don't quite—"

"My life in LA has been a substitute for what I really wanted, which was life and color and someone who..." He paused to suck in some air. This was harder than he'd expected, mostly because she was giving him such a stony stare. "Someone I could love with all my heart."

She stood very still, and her expression didn't change.

"Phil, did you hear what I just said? I love you."

"I heard you. I think I'm probably making this up. It's one of those lucid dreams I've read about."

"Now that you mention it, I'm feeling a little spacey, too. Seventeen hours on the road can do that. But I'm reasonably sure this is real."

"You actually drove here from LA in one hop?"

He rubbed the back of his neck, which was feeling a little stiff. "I know it sounds goofy, but I closed on the house yesterday morning, and...there was no thrill."

"No thrill." She stared at him as if he'd lost his mind.

"I always get a big charge out of turning over the keys to a house I've renovated, but this time I felt nothing. Well, that's not true. I was missing you like the devil. It was a guy and his girlfriend buying it, and I wanted to be them, except you wouldn't have liked the house, because you love this house, and so do I, and—"

"Damon?"

"What?"

"As Rosie says, can we cut to the chase? Exactly why did you come here?"

"To ask you to marry me." Then he stood there stunned, because he'd had *no* idea he was going to blurt that out. But now that he had, he knew it was the most important part of the conversation besides telling her that he loved her.

"Are you sure you know what you're saying? You've been driving a long time, and you might not be completely—"

"Yes, I am absolutely sure." He moved toward her. "Don't you see? That's why I had to drive all this way, immediately, because I knew I wanted you, and there was no time to waste."

"But you said you didn't want to get married, or leave LA, or change your life."

"Because my life was working for me. But now it isn't. My life doesn't work without you, Philomena. I love you and I want—" he spread his arms "—all this."

"Oh, my God." She walked right into his open arms and cradled his face with both hands. "You really mean that, don't you?"

"Of course I mean it." He drew her close and almost moaned out loud with the joy of holding her again. "Otherwise why would I drive seventeen—"

"Hours. Right. I heard you." Smiling, she gazed up at him. "I'll probably be hearing about those seventeen hours on our fiftieth wedding anniversary. *And I drove seventeen hours, blah blah-blah, blah, blah.*"

"Actually it was more like seventeen and a half." Although he didn't want to lose sight of the first part of that comment, the part that made his heart beat faster. "But since you mentioned a fiftieth, it sounds as if you might be interested in my proposal."

"Very interested."

Hot damn. His heart beat even faster. "That must mean that you like me a little bit."

"No."

"No?"

"I like you a whole lot. I might even go so far as to say—" her voice softened "—I love you."

The breath whooshed out of his lungs. "Thank God." He could see it in her eyes, but how he'd wanted to hear her say it.

"I tried really hard not to. I gave the not-loving-you routine all I had, but my heart wouldn't listen. So it's a good thing you showed up because it appears you're the only guy for me."

Joy flooded through him. "That was definitely worth driving seventeen hours to hear."

She cupped the back of his head and drew him down. "Blah, blah-blah, blah, blah."

"Seventy-fifth."

"What?"

"We'll blow right past fifty." As he kissed her, he knew even seventy-five years wouldn't be enough. He'd locked himself away for so long, but Philomena had set him free.

Epilogue

"LET'S TRY THIS AGAIN. Hoist the beer keg one more time for me. I'm sure I'll get the shot this time."

Finn O'Roarke scowled at the blonde behind the camera. Mostly blonde. She'd added lavender streaks to her hair. Chelsea Trask was the most irritating, fascinating woman he'd ever known. He'd met her in line at a Seattle coffee shop four years ago when he'd first hit town.

She'd been kind to a guy fresh off a Wyoming ranch who'd wanted to set up a business in the big city. Her marketing savvy and knowledge of crowdfunding had been invaluable as he'd launched O'Roarke's Brewhouse. He might not have made it without her, and he sent her a check for a percentage of the income every month.

Because of her expertise she'd been the obvious person to consult on Thunder Mountain Academy's Kickstarter project, and she was doing it free of charge. When someone had the brilliant idea to create a Men of Thunder Mountain calendar, she'd insisted Finn had to be in it, and she'd volunteered to handle the photography, since flying to Wyoming for a photo shoot would be ridiculous.

He'd thought he could just pose by the door of his microbrewery, but no, that was too boring for Chelsea. She'd made him dig up his Stetson from the depths of his closet, put on his worn jeans and his scuffed boots while he stood inside the bar with a medium-size keg on his shoulder. And no shirt.

She was fussy about the shot, which didn't surprise him, but holy hell, this was taking forever. He had work to do. Yeah, he kind of enjoyed her contagious enthusiasm, but he had to be careful not to give her the wrong impression. She'd made no bones about the fact that she'd expected him to call after his divorce.

He wasn't calling any woman, at least not until he was certain the microbrewery was solid. He'd learned his lesson—he couldn't tend to a demanding business and be a decent romantic partner at the same time. Maybe some people could, but he wasn't a multitasker. Unfortunately, when he dealt with Chelsea, he often forgot that, so he'd vowed to watch himself.

Hoisting the keg to his shoulder for what he hoped was the last shot, he struck the pose Chelsea had coached him on. She'd complained that he needed a tan, but he didn't spend much time in the great outdoors. And oh, yeah, he had a business to run.

At first she'd threatened to rub some of that self-tanning goop on his chest, but he'd nixed that idea. It was not a manly thing to do, and the thought of Chelsea rubbing stuff on him was way too arousing. She'd grumbled, but had finally decided to use a sepia tone for the finished product so it wouldn't be so obvious that he was pale.

Whatever worked. If the calendar brought in more donations to the academy's Kickstarter fund, he'd pose naked. On second thought, no he wouldn't. The shirtless photo was as far as he was willing to go, especially if Chelsea was taking the pictures.

"Got it!"

He put down the keg with a groan of relief. It wasn't the weight so much as the freezing in place once he'd set it on his shoulder. He was used to carrying the things, not standing around holding them while somebody took a picture.

"That should do the job." Chelsea handed him his shirt before packing up her equipment. "I'll email the file today." She zipped her camera case. "By the way, have you read your email lately?"

He paused in midbutton. "I'm a little behind. Why?"

"Cade and Lexi went over to the Last Chance Ranch last week, and apparently Jack Chance wants to set up a meet-and-greet for potential donors."

"Excellent! That could be really good for the campaign. Thanks for letting me know."

"It wasn't simply an infomercial. The three of them agreed that a professional presentation was in order, so I'm up to bat."

"You're going to the Last Chance Ranch?"

"Bingo." She gazed at him. "They want you to go with me since you're one of the three principals involved."

"Oh." Now there was a potential land mine. He was susceptible to her, but in Seattle he could hide behind his schedule to avoid making another disastrous mistake. That wouldn't be so easy on a trip to Wyoming where they'd be together every day.

"I'll go alone if I have to." She slung her camera bag strap over her shoulder and glanced up at him. "But I don't think that's a good idea. As a former foster kid from the ranch, you'll lend authenticity to my presentation."

She was right, but no surprise there. She was usually right. "Then I guess I'd better go."

"Great! And while we're in the neighborhood, let's drive over to Thunder Mountain Ranch for a few days. After all this effort, I'd love to see it."

Oh, hell. She'd expect him to be her friend and guide on her first-ever experience with ranch living. Keeping a safe distance between them would be almost impossible. "Um, sure, assuming I can be gone that long."

"Jack suggested a weekend in August, and I think we should go with that. Take a look at the email from Cade and let me know when you'd like to fly out. I'll book our flight, and we can settle up later."

"I'll text you."

"That's fine." She paused. "I'm sorry. I put my camera away without showing you those shots. Do you want to see them?"

"No need. I'm sure they're good."

"They are. You're very photogenic." Her gaze held his. "And you look terrific in a Stetson."

The sensual tug he battled told him what kind of trouble he was in. He had a tough time resisting her when they only saw each other a couple of times a month. If they were going to be together 24/7 for nearly a week, all bets were off.

* * * * *

REQUEST YOUR FREE BOOKS!
2 FREE NOVELS PLUS 2 FREE GIFTS!

⊞ HARLEQUIN®

Blaze

red-hot reads!

YES! Please send me 2 FREE Harlequin® Blaze® novels and my 2 FREE gifts (gifts are worth about $10). After receiving them, if I don't wish to receive any more books, I can return the shipping statement marked "cancel." If I don't cancel, I will receive 4 brand-new novels every month and be billed just $4.74 per book in the U.S. or $5.21 per book in Canada. That's a savings of at least 14% off the cover price. It's quite a bargain. Shipping and handling is just 50¢ per book in the U.S. and 75¢ per book in Canada.* I understand that accepting the 2 free books and gifts places me under no obligation to buy anything. I can always return a shipment and cancel at any time. Even if I never buy another book, the two free books and gifts are mine to keep forever.

150/350 HDN GH2D

Name	(PLEASE PRINT)	
Address		Apt. #
City	State/Prov.	Zip/Postal Code

Signature (if under 18, a parent or guardian must sign)

Mail to the **Reader Service:**
IN U.S.A.: P.O. Box 1867, Buffalo, NY 14240-1867
IN CANADA: P.O. Box 609, Fort Erie, Ontario L2A 5X3

Want to try two free books from another line?
Call 1-800-873-8635 or visit www.ReaderService.com.

*Terms and prices subject to change without notice. Prices do not include applicable taxes. Sales tax applicable in N.Y. Canadian residents will be charged applicable taxes. Offer not valid in Quebec. This offer is limited to one order per household. Not valid for current subscribers to Harlequin Blaze books. All orders subject to credit approval. Credit or debit balances in a customer's account(s) may be offset by any other outstanding balance owed by or to the customer. Please allow 4 to 6 weeks for delivery. Offer available while quantities last.

Your Privacy—The Reader Service is committed to protecting your privacy. Our Privacy Policy is available online at www.ReaderService.com or upon request from the Reader Service.

We make a portion of our mailing list available to reputable third parties that offer products we believe may interest you. If you prefer that we not exchange your name with third parties, or if you wish to clarify or modify your communication preferences, please visit us at www.ReaderService.com/consumerchoice or write to us at Reader Service Preference Service, P.O. Box 9062, Buffalo, NY 14240-9062. Include your complete name and address.

HB15

SPECIAL EXCERPT FROM

HARLEQUIN

Blaze

*Police Chief Devin Cassidy can't resist reigniting the
passion between him and Elodie Winchester, even
if it costs him everything—and exposes a shocking
connection to the Quinn family.*

*Here's a sneak preview of
THE MIGHTY QUINNS: DEVIN,
the latest steamy installment in*
Kate Hoffmann's
beloved miniseries
THE MIGHTY QUINNS.

Elodie hurried downstairs and threw open the front door.
She stepped out into the storm, running across the lawn.
When she reached the police cruiser, she stopped. "What
are you doing out here?" she shouted above the wind.

Dev slowly got out of the car, his hand braced along the
top of the door. "I couldn't sleep."

"I couldn't, either," she shouted.

It was all he needed. He stepped toward her and before
she knew it, she was in his arms, his hands smoothing over
the rain-soaked fabric of her dress. His lips covered hers in
a desperate, deeply powerful kiss. He molded her mouth to
his, still searching for something even more intimate.

The fabric of her dress clung to her naked skin, a feeble
barrier to his touch. Elodie fought the urge to reach for the
hem of her dress and pull it over her head. They were on a
public street, with houses all around.

"Come with me," she murmured. She laced her fingers through his and pulled him toward the house.

Once they reached the protection of the veranda, he grabbed her waist again, pulling her into another kiss. Dev smoothed his hand up her torso until he found her breast and he cupped it, his thumb teasing at her taut nipple.

Elodie reached for the hem of his shirt, but it was tucked underneath his leather utility belt. "Take this off," she murmured, frantically searching for the buckle.

He carefully unclipped his gun and set it on a nearby table. A moment later, his utility belt dropped to the ground, followed by his badge and, finally, his shirt. Her palms skimmed over hard muscle and smooth skin. His shoulders, once slight, were now broad, his torso a perfect V.

Dev reached for the hem of her dress and bunched it in his fists, pulling it higher and higher until it was twisted around her waist. He gently pushed her back against the door and she moaned as his fingertips skimmed the soft skin of her inner thigh.

Wild sensations raced through her body and she trembled as she anticipated what would come next…

Don't miss
THE MIGHTY QUINNS: DEVIN by Kate Hoffmann,
available August 2015 wherever
Harlequin® Blaze® books and ebooks are sold.

www.Harlequin.com

THE WORLD IS BETTER WITH

Romance

Harlequin has everything from contemporary, passionate and heartwarming to suspenseful and inspirational stories.

Whatever your mood,
we have a romance just for you!